Not Talented
in Hollywood

Leonie Gant

ISBN-13: 978-0-9942990-6-2

Dedication

To my parents.
Thank you for teaching me the value of persistence.

Chapter One

The darkness of the theater did nothing to disguise the fact that we were sitting in a very small space. As a small community theater, it had less than one hundred seats to be filled. Unfortunately at this moment, there was a grand total of nine people in the audience. I knew this because I had counted them as a distraction from the show that I was being forced to watch. Another unfortunate point was that the group I was with made up four of those nine people. I'm not really a big theater goer. My pretensions of culture kind of begin and end with a big budget science fiction or action movie. I'm really one of those people who wants to be entertained. I don't want to have to actually think.

Spending a Saturday evening in a theater is not exactly something that I would go out of my way to do. Tonight though, I was supporting a friend. In fact, we were all here to support a friend. Edwin lives in my apartment complex with my friend, Crystal, our landlady, Miss Betsy, and our teenage project, Sean. This was not the first time we had attended a play that Edwin had performed in. He was an aspiring actor, determined to work his way up into the movies. He was the hardest working person I knew. He kept taking temp jobs to earn his way and he also took any part in any production, no matter how small, to perfect his craft. By all rights and if the universe was fair, his big break should be just around the corner.

Unfortunately, Edwin Litchfield was also one of the worst actors that I had ever seen and some of the theater groups I had been forced to sit through had contained some very ordinary acting. Edwin had started off as a model in his home country of England and that suited him. The guy was impossibly gorgeous, tall with a defined body, blonde wavy hair and deep blue eyes that a woman could drown in. Modeling bored him so he decided that the next natural step was acting. I used to believe that acting was easy and that anyone could do it. It isn't until you see someone who is genuinely, excruciatingly bad at it that you appreciate that there may actually be some talent behind the ability to act. My friend, Crystal, works in her father's casting agency. She lives in fear of the day that Edwin asks her to help him get a real acting job. I know he won't. Edwin has a major crush on Crystal and he knows that she is hit on by unknown actors, often purely for her connections. He has some noble idea in his head that he can make it without her help. Once he breaks through and becomes a star, he intends to seriously pursue her. I think he's an idiot and I have told him that it is a ridiculous plan. Male pride is a tricky thing though and sometimes you just withdraw from the argument as you are just butting your head against a brick wall.

I felt an elbow hit me sharply in the ribs and glared at Crystal. She was small but I'd learned from previous experience that she could pack a punch when she wanted to.

"Wake up, Trudie," she hissed as the curtains went down.

"I was awake," I whispered back, rubbing my side.

"Are you sure? You didn't twitch for like a full five minutes, that's usually a sign that you're fast asleep."

I glared at her. I wish I could argue the fact but she was right. I cannot stay still for any length of time. I always need to be moving or unconscious. I really don't have an in between state.

"Is it finished?" I asked.

"Yes," she groaned as the curtain came up again and we started clapping as loudly as we could to hide the fact that most of the seats were empty.

Sean leaned over. "I am not coming to another one of these. I don't care what you threaten me with," he said with all the whining petulance that only a teenage boy can muster.

This time I had threatened to cut off his supply of homemade cookies. I had recently taken some time off work and gone on a baking binge. Thankfully, having a teenage boy around meant I had a ready customer and nothing went to waste. I frowned. I really should be getting back to work. I had taken some time off on the advice of Crystal who thought I needed to relax and find myself away from the stress of my job. I work for the very wealthy who are lacking the ability to deal with staff on any kind of level. My job is to be the personal assistant to people who alienate the dedicated employees who work for them. This kind of work takes an extraordinary patience and the ability to stop talking before you tell someone the truth. I do that well. However, my last few jobs had managed to push those stress levels through the roof.

Miss Betsy leaned over from her seat on the other side of Crystal.

"So what are we telling him this time?" she asked as we all looked expectantly at Crystal.

Being a casting agent, Crystal was well versed in letting people down with as little damage to their ego as was humanly possible. In an industry where people seemed to pride themselves on how cruelly they could destroy someone's dreams, Crystal was able to gently guide people to their full potential.

She was thoughtful for a second. "I've got nothing," she said, grimacing.

I could understand what she was talking about. Edwin was our friend but watching him act was a truly painful experience. It would be better if we could see some improvement, any improvement. In the year we had been coming to these plays, there had been no progress and it was becoming harder to watch. We would, of course. If Edwin wanted to continue with this dream, then we would support him. It was just difficult knowing that he was never going to achieve it.

"I'm going to take this one home," Miss Betsy interrupted, looking pointedly at Sean.

"Why did I have to sit through that torture and now I have to miss out on the party?" Sean complained.

"Because you've got homework and you've been having trouble with your algebra lately," Miss Betsy said sternly.

Sean looked at me pleadingly.

"Not going to work on me," I said airily. He pouted in that way that sixteen year old boys have, before following meekly behind Miss Betsy.

"He's been getting a little bit harder to deal with lately, especially while you were gone," Crystal said.

I snorted. If Crystal thought Sean was hard to deal with, she really didn't have a clue. I had just come back from a three month placement with an eighteen year old pop star on tour. On my first day he tried to get me to carry his drugs through an airport. When I refused he threw a temper tantrum that would have made a two year old proud. When that didn't change my mind, he decided to get his father and mother to deal with me. Doing his best to disprove Darwin's theory that only the fittest survive to propagate the species, the teenager's father threw his own temper tantrum, which worsened the calmer I was.

Fortunately for me, I had been hired by the record company and not the client. I was being paid very well to do my job and to try to limit the excesses of this particular pop star and his massive entourage. I had signed on for three months and I completed that three months despite the entire entourage doing their best to get rid of me. People who live their lives on the coat tails of a spoiled brat do not react well when you are trying to pull back on the gravy train. At the end of the tour the record company tried to get me to extend the contract and work permanently in that role. I would have preferred to have my eyes poked out than spend any more time with that particular client. He was just as happy as I was when that placement had come to an end. I was now taking a well-earned break before taking on another client.

"Oh, of course," said Crystal, "your runaway job."

"I did not run away," I said, annoyed at the change in conversation.

"Please, you ran so fast and so far because you didn't want to face him."

"We're not talking about this," I said, gathering up my purse.

"He came by your apartment," Crystal said.

"Please, can we not talk about this?" I pleaded. I really did not want to talk about what may or may not have been the biggest mistake I had ever made.

Crystal looked at me knowingly but wisely held her tongue. I had been a coward. Three months ago I had walked away from Detective Jake Griffin and grabbed the first out of town job that I was offered. At the time I had been convinced of the rightness of my actions. He was a dedicated officer who was single minded in his approach to his job. Nothing came between him and being a cop, not even the tentative thing that we had started. I had not wanted to come in second to his career, so thought the best thing for me to do was walk away and make a clean break before I got too involved.

Three months later and I might not be happy with my decision but I had made peace with it. That didn't mean that I was particularly proud of my actions and Crystal knew that.

"Thank you." I was relieved when she stopped talking. "Now it's time to put on your game face so we can get down there and tell Edwin how proud we are of him."

"Proud of what?" she asked skeptically, obviously remembering the hour and a half of fairly ordinary acting we had just sat through.

"That he has the courage to go after his dream, no matter what," I said.

"Right, that." Crystal plastered on a smile at the same time I did.

Chapter Two

Getting backstage wasn't difficult. Hearing the vitriol coming from behind the door, however, was. The director obviously had decided that the performance was not up to her expected standard, and was letting the cast know in quite loud and explicit language. Hesitating to open the door, I looked at Crystal.

"That's Catarina Badal." Crystal must have noticed my confusion. "She's kind of fallen pretty far."

That was an understatement. Ten years ago Catarina Badal was the artistic prodigy of directing in Hollywood. Her debut low budget movie had come from nowhere and had been a critical and box office smash. Her second movie had won her a host of awards including an Oscar. Since then though her movies had become more and more bizarre. I hadn't heard anything about her for a couple of years. I had to say that finding her directing in a community theater was a bit of a surprise.

I felt Crystal stiffen beside me. Catarina had just started giving a rather blistering critique of Edwin's performance. I put my arm out to stop Crystal from storming in there. She looked at me fiercely. Crystal is my best friend. She is tiny. When not walking around in her favored four inch high stilettos, she doesn't quite make five feet. Despite her lack of size, when it comes to the people she cares about, she is like a vicious little Pomeranian who has no fear when it comes to taking on a Rottweiler. I always worry that one day that Rottweiler is going to bite back.

"Don't," I whispered. "If Edwin thinks you heard that he will be humiliated."

Crystal stopped as my words got through to her and nodded her head. We stepped back, away from the door, waiting for the tirade to be over. The door swung open and Catarina Badal charged through with barely a look in our direction.

"What are you doing here?" she snarled as she saw me first. I stumbled as I tried to find something to say but it was too late. Her gaze had swung to Crystal and just like magic, her attitude changed. She held her hand out to Crystal and oozed friendliness.

"Crystal Bronstein, it is so good to see you. You're working with your father now aren't you?"

Crystal had put on her work face. That one that looks polite and interested, but because I know her so well, I know that it means she is fully aware of how fake the person talking to her really is and she's not falling for it at all. Crystal's father ran the biggest casting agency in town. He is considered one of those powerful people in Hollywood who can make or break careers. As his only child, Crystal had learned very early that most people were only nice to her based on what her father could do for them.

Catarina Badal grabbed Crystal's hand as if they were the oldest of friends. "I would love to catch up with you," she said as she started dragging Crystal along.

"Actually," said Crystal, extricating herself. "I'm here to see Edwin Litchfield."

Catarina stopped as if she'd been struck. "Well I guess that's one way for him to get a job. God knows, he wouldn't based on his acting." With a derisive look at Crystal she stalked off.

Stepping up I grabbed hold of Crystal around the waist as she went to take off after the director.

"Don't do it," I warned.

You'd think I'd have a lot more trouble holding on to a squirming woman, but surprisingly enough, over the last year of knowing Crystal, my technique had been honed well. I just needed to remember if she started kicking, those stilettos hurt badly.

"I'm going to kill her," hissed Crystal.

"No, you're not," I said.

"Okay, maybe I won't kill her but I'm going to destroy her career."

I pointedly looked around the theater we were standing in. "You may be a bit late for that. Looks like she did a good enough job herself."

Crystal stopped squirming and looked back at me, a short bark of laughter coming from her.

"So, is this my opening night gift?" drawled Edwin from the doorway.

We both looked over to him and our faces must have shown our confusion. He waved his hand at us and at the same time we realized exactly how we must look. I had my arm around Crystal's waist as her back was plastered to my chest. As she'd been trying to get away, my taller body was slightly bent over hers, and at that moment we both blushed.

"I'm not saying I don't like it," said Edwin. "I mean, I know that flowers are traditional, but if this is how you were planning to go, you could at least have waited until I got here."

I quickly let go of Crystal and stepped back. Crystal stumbled on her heels and Edwin pushed forward to hold her up.

"That wasn't what it looked like," she said as Edwin straightened her.

"Oh, I prefer to think that it was exactly what it looked like." Edwin smiled down at her. Crystal blushed and Edwin grinned wider. "So, were you going to tell me what that was about?" Edwin asked.

"No, I don't think so," Crystal said slowly.

"Well then, I will go back to my version," he said.

Crystal balled up her fist and hit him in the stomach.

"Oh," he gasped. "I think you wounded me with your tiny, tiny fist."

"You are such an idiot," she said, smiling as she swept past him into the backstage area.

"After you," Edwin said to me as he waved his hand in front of him.

The party was small but the cast and crew seemed to be having a lot of fun, especially since Catarina had left. Of course, the second Crystal walked into the room, everyone wanted to be her new best friend. No one is quite as popular at a community theater event as a famous Hollywood casting agent. Throughout the night I slowly got pushed further and further away from the center of the action.

"How are you doing?" Edwin asked, handing me a drink as we watched Crystal hold court.

"Not too bad," I said. "Crystal seems to be having fun.

"Nothing like a group of unemployed actors who want to make it big," Edwin said, with a little bitterness.

"You okay?" I asked, putting down the drink and really looking at him. I had been away for three months with my pop brat job and had only been back for a few days. With Edwin in rehearsals, I hadn't seen him much, but there was a tension in him that I'd never seen before. He pushed his hand through his hair.

"I don't think I'm going to make it, Trudie," he said softly.

"Why not?"

"I'm not very good." Edwin stared intently at his drink. "I know that. I thought I'd get better, but I just don't feel it."

"Maybe it isn't for you, maybe your heart isn't in it," I said sympathetically.

"I notice you didn't say that I was getting better, regardless of what I think."

I winced. Edwin put his hand on mine.

"No, Trudie, don't feel bad. I value your honesty."

I leaned into him and put my head on his shoulder.

"I think you're amazing for going after it the way you have. I would never tell you to stop or that you weren't good enough."

"I know, Trudie, but I think I need to get a dose of reality."

I straightened up. "Maybe you need to look at what you really want. What are you passionate about?"

I followed Edwin's eyes as they turned towards Crystal, the longing in them almost painful to watch.

I nudged him in the side. "Ask her out, tell her how you feel," I urged.

"I can't," he said. "Not until I've sorted myself out." He took another drink from his bottle. "What I can do first is to realize I am never going to make it as an actor." He stood up suddenly.

"What are you doing?" I asked.

"I'm going to tell Catarina that she's right. I'm never going to make it, so I'm quitting."

Putting down his bottle, he strode purposefully out of the room. I saw Crystal watch him as he left. Taking another mouthful of my drink, my attention was quickly taken by one of the other actors, who finding that he couldn't get close to Crystal had decided her friend was an acceptable second choice. Tiring quickly of my monosyllabic answers to his questions about Crystal, he wandered off and Crystal left her adoring court to sit with me. I eyed her over my drink.

"So exactly how privileged am I that you've decided to grace me with your presence?"

Crystal elbowed me in the side.

"Ouch," I groaned. "What was that for?"

"For being an idiot," she said. "Where did Edwin go?"

"To tell Catarina that he was quitting as he wasn't a good enough actor and he never would be."

Crystal gaped at me. "What are we doing sitting here then?" she said, grabbing my hand.

"We're letting him be an adult and make his own way in life," I said.

"Of all the stupid ideas. He's making a massive life change. He needs us with him."

Not having any choice in the matter, I let myself get dragged off in search of Edwin. Crystal, having virtually lived in these kinds of theaters all her life, unerringly found the director's office. The door was closed. She went to grab the door handle and I grabbed hold of her wrist.

"We can't just go in there," I said. "What if they're still talking?"

Crystal pressed her ear to the door. "I don't hear anything," she said as she grabbed the door handle again, rolling her eyes as I reached over and knocked on the door.

"Catarina," she called out. "We're just looking for..."

Crystal stopped and over her head I saw the reason why. Catarina Badal was slumped over her desk and in the middle of her back was a knife that looked disturbingly like the prop knife that had earlier in the night been used to kill Edwin in his painful death scene. Crystal gaped as I raced over to check the pulse. I would like to say that my abilities in an emergency carried me through the shocking scene. However, this wasn't the first body that I had seen and I think that I had become a little desensitized. That was a disturbing thought. I couldn't find a pulse and I pulled out my phone to call emergency when Crystal found her voice.

"Stop."

I froze. "What are you talking about?" I asked.

"If we walk out right now, nobody needs to know we were in here," she said.

I must have looked at her strangely.

"I don't want you involved," she said, concern all over her face.

It may sound callous but in the last six months I had found a total of two dead bodies. I had also been shot once, threatened several times, and almost killed in a fire. Crystal did not have the greatest family life and, for whatever reason, Edwin and I were as close to family for her as her father was. I knew she was just trying to protect me.

"We're already involved," I said quietly. "We were looking for Edwin, your fingerprints are on the door. We found the body, we have to call the cops."

Crystal looked as if she was going to start arguing, but then we heard a scream behind her and a thud. One of the actresses was out cold on the floor.

"No going back now." I punched in the familiar number. "I really should put this on speed dial," I muttered grimly.

Voices reached us as people who had heard the scream came running, including Edwin. Looking in, he saw the body, and grabbed Crystal and held her.

"What's going on?" he asked quietly.

"We came looking for you and found Catarina like this," Crystal mumbled in his shirt.

"She was fine ten minutes ago," he said. "I was just talking to her."

"Great," I said. "You were probably the last person to see her alive."

"That's not a good thing is it?" said Edwin.

"No," I said, with the voice of experience. "It isn't."

Chapter Three

As the small theater filled up with paramedics and police, the three of us sat to the side. Crystal and I sat on either side of Edwin, trying to talk him through it.

"Who would want to kill her?" asked Edwin, shaking his head.

Crystal looked at me and I winced, her threat to kill the woman only an hour ago was still going through my head.

"You have got to be kidding me."

I looked up to see what Crystal was looking at, only to see Detective Jake Griffin and his partner Detective Liza Ramos studying us from across the room.

"This can't be good," mumbled Edwin.

"Seriously," said Crystal. "Are there no other cops in this city?"

I felt an overwhelming need to escape. Seeing the two of them talking to the uniformed officers who had arrived previously, I could feel the anxiety rising in me. Crystal looked at me worriedly.

"I'm fine," I said.

"Honey, you are so far from fine it isn't funny," she said.

"No really, I'm the one who decided it wouldn't work. My decision, I'm not second guessing myself now."

"Well, it looks like he's not willing to face you yet either," Edwin said.

I looked up to see Griffin's back as he went into the room where Catarina's body was still lying. Ramos headed towards us and I gave her a small smile of recognition. Stopping before us she looked directly at me.

"You know, seeing you here is really not the best way for me to end a bad day."

"I'm sorry," I ventured, my voice rising in a question,

thinking that the sooner I finished with her, the sooner I could go home. I really needed to work on those reasons that I had walked away from Griffin three months earlier.

"You found the body?" said Ramos.

"Yes we did," piped in Crystal. "We knocked on her office door. When we didn't hear anything we walked in and found her like that."

"Why were you down here? Wasn't the party upstairs?"

Crystal and I looked worriedly at Edwin.

"They were looking for me," he said.

"Why down here?" Ramos asked.

"I came to tell Catarina that I was quitting."

"Was this before or after she called you a no talent disaster who would never be able to get anywhere in this business unless the casting couch was still in force."

I winced. I hadn't heard that part of the tirade.

Edwin's face flushed a deep red. "After."

"So it would be fair to say you were angry with Miss Badal," Ramos continued questioning in that bored voice of hers.

"I wasn't angry, just a little upset."

"Upset enough to put a knife into her back?"

"Hey, wait a minute," said Crystal.

"You can't possibly be thinking that Edwin did this," I burst out.

"That's ridiculous, Edwin is the gentlest, kindest..." Crystal said indignantly.

"I'm sure he is," said Ramos. "However, he was also the last person to see her alive and she had just torn strips off of him in front of everyone. Makes him a viable suspect and he needs to come down to the station with us to answer some questions."

Holding up her hand she pointed at Crystal and me.

"You two are just going to make things harder for him if you get in the way."

"It's okay," said Edwin as he stood up.

Crystal gripped his hand.

"I'll be fine. I didn't do it. I just need to sort this out."

Crystal and I stood up and gave him a hug. The uniform officer came and took him away and Crystal started organizing a lawyer on her phone for him. Ramos pulled me aside.

"I need you to do something," she said.

"What?" I asked, unused to Ramos speaking to me without an interrogation room being involved.

"Whatever is going on between you and Griffin, I need you to fix it."

"I'm pretty sure that is none of your business, and I'm absolutely sure it has nothing to do with this case, or the fact that you have just taken my friend into custody for something there is no way that he did," I said, feeling a bit annoyed.

"Actually, it is my business. This thing the two of you have going on was fun to watch when it started. I'll admit that I enjoyed the way you shook him up, but whatever you did is not funny anymore. It's messing with my days."

"So, it's all about you is it?" I said, gritting my teeth.

"When it makes my life difficult it is, now fix it," she said.

"There is nothing to fix," I said. "And I would really appreciate you keeping out of it."

I turned around and stalked towards Crystal.

"What's wrong?" she asked.

I raised an eyebrow at her.

"I mean, other than the fact we found a dead body and Edwin is up to his neck in it," she amended.

"Nothing else important. Have you managed to get a lawyer for Edwin?"

She nodded. "My dad's criminal lawyer is going to meet Edwin at the station. He'll make sure he doesn't do or say anything that's going to get him in any more trouble than he is already."

I could see the tension in her as she held herself stiffly. Crystal is one of the strongest people I have ever met and

I know her well. In that moment I could tell she was barely hanging on. If there is anything that frustrates her, it is being unable to help someone she cares about. As much as she would deny it to anyone, I knew that she cared about Edwin very much.

"Do you want to go down to the station and wait for him?" I asked gently.

"No, I know that would be hard for you, what with Griffin there and everything," she said, but I could see that she wanted to.

"It doesn't matter. This mess with Griffin is my fault, not yours and not Edwin's. I'll deal with it, but if you need to be there I'll take you."

Crystal flung her arms around me and I knew that it was just as much to hide the tears in her eyes as it was a gesture of gratitude.

"Please, I need to be there. I don't ever want him to think that he's alone."

"He's not alone," I said, hugging her back. "He's got us, he could never be alone."

Chapter Four

Sitting in the police station waiting area, I was glad we had come. Crystal sat there, gnawing impatiently on her lip. I had never seen her like this. Crystal was the product of a marriage between a big time Hollywood casting agent and a Las Vegas showgirl who hung around long enough to get pregnant and guarantee herself a big payday. Crystal's mother had used her as a bargaining chip for ever-increasing payments from her father in exchange for custody, all the time ignoring her daughter in favor of a fast moving line of husbands. At last count Crystal had seen her way through nine stepfathers. As a result Crystal had every right to be a bitter person, twisted by the mercenary nature of her mother. Instead she had ended up a warm, loving person who adored her father and was fiercely loyal to her friends. On the flip side of that, she did not cope well when anything threatened those she cared about. Of course, in reality, not many of us do. When Crystal's lawyer came out with an exhausted looking Edwin, Crystal jumped up and I could see that she was desperate to hug him, but she stood back and made me do it first. Just so she could fool herself and everyone else into believing that she only did it as a friend. The only person she was fooling was Edwin.

The lawyer cleared his throat. "Mr Litchfield is free to go at this stage. The police are still treating him as a suspect."

I peered over Edwin's shoulder to see Griffin leaning against a wall, studying me with an unwavering stare. For an instant I was caught in those green eyes, and memories washed through me of how it had felt to be held in his strong arms and to feel his lips on mine. Wrenching my eyes away I directed my question to the lawyer.

"Is there anything that we can do to help him?"

"At this moment, just keep his head down. Don't do anything stupid like let him bolt. The fact that he's a British citizen and can go home at a moment's notice has a tendency to make cops a bit twitchy. Do something stupid that looks like he is heading out of the country and they might arrest him, even if they don't have enough evidence. Just keep calm and don't do anything stupid."

At that both Edwin and Crystal looked in my direction. Unfairly I might add. My previous history may have suggested that I did stupid things but that was untrue. I just sometimes found myself in stupid situations.

"Got it, no stupid," I mumbled.

The lawyer roughly clapped Edwin on the shoulder. "Remember, keep your head down and don't speak to the cops unless I'm there."

Picking up his briefcase he left the three of us standing there.

"Ready to get out of here?" I said to Edwin with a forced cheeriness.

Edwin switched his attention between me and the detective who was still watching us intently.

"I think that might be a really good idea," he said.

Driving home, the car was filled with a tense silence. Edwin obviously didn't want to talk about his experience and Crystal and I weren't going to push him. As the three of us separated into our own homes at the complex, I noticed that Crystal was following me.

"We need to talk," she whispered as she hustled me into my apartment.

"What are you doing?" I asked, pulling my arm away from her vise like grip.

"I'm going to ask you for a favor and I want you to think about it before dismissing it out of hand," Crystal said calmly.

Her mild tone was in direct contrast to the panic that I could see growing in her eyes.

"You know I'd do anything for you," I said gently, hoping to head off the meltdown I could see coming.

Crystal smiled tightly. "I need you to sleep with Griffin," she said.

Admittedly not what I was expecting. Even for Crystal, that was a strange request. I waited for her to tell me she was joking. Unfortunately she looked deadly serious.

"Why on earth do you want me to sleep with Griffin?" I asked incredulously.

"Come on," Crystal said. "We all saw the way he was looking at you, Trudie. He still wants you, and if you'd just give it up I think you can convince him that Edwin is innocent and he'll leave him alone." She looked hopeful as only someone with the most insane of plans can.

I really couldn't think what to say. Sure, Crystal was a little nutty at times but this one easily topped any of the other schemes she had tried to talk me into. I put my hands on her shoulders, maneuvered her to the couch and sat her down.

"Crystal, think for a moment," I said, with more patience than that suggestion deserved. "I stopped seeing Griffin because I don't believe he could ever put me before his work. He is completely dedicated to being a cop. I really don't think that one roll in the hay with me is going to cause a complete change in his personality."

"You could be underestimating yourself," Crystal said desperately.

"No, I'm not and I think you know it too."

Crystal put her head in her hands and quietly started crying. I put an arm around her shoulder and hugged her, letting her cry it out while murmuring all the nonsensical things you're supposed to say at a moment like this.

"I can't lose him, Trudie. I…I think I'm in love with him."

"Of course you are, you idiot," I said gently.

Crystal looked up. "What do you mean?"

"Anyone with eyes can see you're in love with him."

Crystal stiffened. "Does Edwin know?"

"No," I said. "I'm pretty sure that Edwin doesn't know."

"I just, I love him and I would do anything to help him," Crystal sniffed.

"So glad that you doing anything to help him includes pimping me out," I said dryly.

Crystal clapped a hand over her mouth and a small giggle came out.

"I'm so sorry, but we were at the station and the way he was looking at you. I just started thinking that if his feelings for you were so strong, maybe we could use it to Edwin's advantage."

"You know, Crystal, there are moments when your thinking truly concerns me," I said.

"I blame my mother," Crystal said. "Only lesson she ever taught me was when you're backed into a corner, sex can always get you out."

"My mom said to go for the eyes, throat and groin," I said as I got up to get a coffee.

"I think I prefer your mom," Crystal said.

"Of course you do."

My mom had stayed with me for a while, about five months ago, after I had been shot in the case where I first met Griffin. With my mother's instinct for finding and fixing broken people, she had latched onto Crystal and smothered her with all the maternal devotion that was normally reserved for her three children. Crystal had lapped up the attention and was now a fervent follower of my mother's words of questionable wisdom.

"What are we going to do?" Crystal said, in that small voice of hers.

"Why don't we let the police handle it?" I said gently, handing her a cup of coffee.

"But what if they get it wrong? What if they start to really think that Edwin did it?"

"And what if, while you're worrying here, they find out

who did it? Let them do their job, Crystal. Just be here for him, talk to him. Let him know that you're with him the whole way."

"You could be right," said Crystal doubtfully. "I'm so sorry. I don't know what I was thinking, trying to get you to sleep with Griffin. He was pretty intense at the station. I thought he was going to come over and throw you over his shoulder and take you away."

I grimaced at the image Crystal presented, but couldn't deny the flutter in the pit of my stomach at the thought.

"I think you may be overstating things," I said.

"I don't think so," said Crystal. "While you were trying very hard to avoid looking at him, I was watching. He did not look like a man ready to give up on what he wants and I hate to be the one to tell you, but he wants you."

"I can't do it," I whispered, looking intently at my coffee cup.

"Then don't," said Crystal. "You've avoided him for the last three months. Tonight was one of those situations. With any luck you won't see him again."

I nodded, hoping that luck would be on my side for once.

"Although," Crystal smirked, "we'll keep the sleeping with him plan in reserve for now. You know, just in case."

Chapter Five

I wish I could say that those words did not keep me up that night. I really wish I could say that it was my worrying about Edwin that caused me to get up really early the next morning, after giving up on trying to get a decent night's sleep. By that time I had convinced myself of a lot of things. Top of my list was that Edwin was going to be fine and second on my list was that I had made the right decision with Griffin. If the man could cause this much chaos to my psyche, just by looking at me, then it was better that I kept as far away from him as possible. Of course, answering my door and finding the one person in this world I wanted to keep my distance from, didn't help me in my hopes for a peaceful day. Standing in the doorway was Detective Jake Griffin, looking just as tired as I felt. Of course that didn't detract from the fact that he still looked good.

"Planning on inviting me in?" he asked as I stood there gaping like an idiot.

"Oh, of course," I said, years of my mother's etiquette training coming to the fore.

I tugged on my shirt as I closed the door, painfully aware that I was wearing my combination of clothes which, while very comfortable, left a great deal to be desired in the style stakes. I followed Griffin into the living area to find him pacing the floor. Never having seen him as anything other than totally in control of his environment, I was surprised.

"What are you doing here?" I asked.

He stopped. "Why have you been avoiding me?"

Alrighty then, straight to the heart of the matter.

"We talked about this," I said as gently as I could. "We're just not right for each other."

"No, I remember pretty clearly that you said that my job meant more to me than you could and you walked away and disappeared for a few months. We never actually got a chance to talk about it, because I have a few things to say."

I clasped my hands together and waited. He was right, I did bolt without giving him a chance to have closure.

Griffin resumed pacing, his hand raking through his dark hair as he pinned me in place with that green eyed stare of his.

"I was really angry with you until I realized that this is your problem, not mine," he said.

Wait a second, this didn't sound like closure and I opened my mouth to argue.

"No," he said, holding a hand up. "My turn remember. You are so messed up by your ex-fiancé that you are not willing to give anyone else another chance."

I opened my mouth.

"Still my turn," he said, holding a finger up as if to emphasize the point.

"See, you act practical and calm. It fools people into believing you are in complete control of your emotions. You could tell that there was something real happening between us, so you grabbed onto the first excuse to run away from it."

"You finished?" I asked, starting to get annoyed at the character assassination.

"Not by a long shot, honey," he said, and I could see his eyes sparking with the excitement of a challenge.

"What is between us is real and I am not going to let you throw it away because you're too scared to grab onto a good thing."

He stalked towards me and I could see his eyes sparking with something else now. Despite my best intentions I backed away from him, not stopping until I felt the wall at my back. He dipped his head and softly touched his lips to mine. I moaned at the contact. I had missed this so much. Even when I was telling myself he was no good for me, I would remember how it felt to have him holding and kissing me. I had never felt this before and I was very afraid that I would never feel it again.

"See," he whispered against my lips. "This is what's between us. You can't deny it and I don't want to deny it. I have spent three months in agony, missing you," he said hoarsely, and despite the strength in his words I could see that letting himself be this vulnerable was costing him. But he was doing it, and in that moment I crumbled. I sought out his lips and poured all the feelings that I had been burying for the last few months into that kiss. It was his turn to groan and he took over the kiss, deepening it. Feeling his arms wrap around me, I felt at peace and on fire all at the same time. I started to lose track of everything but those lips caressing mine.

"Oh my God." I heard Crystal's voice as Griffin pulled away from me. Sure enough, there was Crystal standing at the door, her eyes wide and yes, there was the beginning of a smile.

Griffin looked down at me and I noticed that even though he had pulled away from the kiss, his arms were still wrapped around me, seemingly unwilling to let me go.

"This discussion isn't finished," he pitched his voice low as he gave me a squeeze before letting go.

Watching him walk out the door, I was finally able to acknowledge that I was in a lot of trouble when it came to Jake Griffin. When he was out of sight, Crystal looked back at me, taking in my obviously swollen lips and messed up clothing.

"Way to take one for the team," she said, grinning. "Last night I figured there was no chance but here I find you sacrificing yourself for your friends."

"You quite finished?" I asked dryly.

"Oh, I don't think I'm ever going to let you forget about this moment," she grinned.

"It's not what you're thinking," I said.

"I don't know. I walked in here and there you are about to climb Mount Griffin, if I don't miss my guess."

"That reminds me," I said, "I want my key back."

"You gave it to me," she said, smiling.

"For emergency situations," I stressed.

"This was an emergency," she said, still with that grin on her face.

"In the strictest definition of the term?" I queried.

"Okay, maybe not an emergency as such."

I stood there looking at her, not saying a word.

"I went to Edwin's place to talk and he's not there. I thought he might have come over here for breakfast."

"No, as you can see I'm quite alone."

Now it was Crystal's turn to look at me with an amused expression on her face.

"Well I was alone until Griffin showed up." And kissed me in a way that I was never going to get over.

"I'm worried about him." Crystal slumped on my couch.

"We're all worried about him," I said.

"He looked so lost last night, as if he didn't know what to do next. Did Griffin say anything about the case?" she asked hopefully.

"No, I hadn't got to the interrogation part of your evil plan," I said.

"Maybe next time," said Crystal. "Don't give me that look because believe me, there is going to be a next time."

I dropped my head as I walked away because she was right.

"Where are you going?" she called out as I went in my bedroom.

"I'm getting dressed. I'm assuming you want to go and look for Edwin."

"Good plan. Do you have anything for breakfast? I've run out of food at my place."

Crystal was always running out of food at her place. Between her, Sean and Edwin, my grocery bills were at least triple what they should be. I was amazed they hadn't starved while I was away.

Once Crystal had been fed and I finally looked like I could be seen in public, we went looking for Edwin. We found Miss Betsy working in the garden as usual.

"Have you seen Edwin today?" Crystal asked.

Miss Betsy straightened up, took off her hat and wiped her forehead.

"Oh yes, he took Sean surfing this morning. Those boys were up at the crack of dawn."

I wasn't surprised. Sean and Edwin had bonded over their mutual love of the sport. I liked the fact Sean had managed to find a decent male role model after the disaster of a boyfriend that his mother had brought home.

Heading for the beach, Crystal and I found Edwin sitting on the sand, looking out at the ocean. Each of us sat on either side of him.

"Where's Sean?" I asked, looking out over the water.

"He's still out there," Edwin said, waving his hand in the general direction of the ocean.

"I think he met a girl and he's out there surfing with her. Seems I was cramping his style."

Crystal and I smiled. Sean had the hormones of any sixteen year old boy and he was always meeting girls. His goofy sense of humor, red hair and freckles seemed to appeal to teenage girls and he was learning to capitalize on it.

Crystal nudged Edwin with her shoulder. "So, are you going to tell us what's going on or are we going to have to play twenty questions?"

"Just trying to work out what I want to do with my life."

Crystal frowned, "I thought you wanted to be an actor."

Edwin sighed heavily. "I don't know if I ever really wanted to be an actor. I started off modeling when I was seventeen. Made money early so I didn't bother going to school. Next thing, I find I'm completely bored with modeling, but I don't have much of an education. Acting seemed to be the next logical step. Now I'm looking at it and I suck at acting. I really don't want to go back to posing in front of a camera."

I looked at him worriedly. The poor guy actually looked really down.

"How about sucking it up and dealing with it."

My head dropped. I loved Crystal but she really didn't do sympathy well.

"So you finally realized that acting isn't your thing. At least you worked it out now rather than twenty years' time. Now is the time for you to man up and work out what you want to do with the rest of life. Sitting around looking at the ocean isn't going to get you anywhere."

Keeping in mind that this was the man that only twelve hours previously Crystal had confessed to loving, I was a bit surprised at the tirade. I could tell that Edwin was a little shocked too.

"You want to kick the boot in a bit harder," he said through tightly clenched teeth as he got up from the sand.

"Where are you going?" I called out as he stalked off.

"Obviously nowhere," said Edwin. "Give Sean a ride home will you."

With that he turned around and left us in the sand.

"What the hell are you trying to do?" I asked Crystal incredulously.

"He needed some motivation," she said calmly.

"Motivation, yes. A kick in the teeth, not so much."

"He'll be fine, trust me. I know Edwin. If we let him wallow, he'll do it for ages. This way he gets a kick in the pants and he'll work out what he needs to do that much quicker. I need him to work it out so he can realize that I'm the woman for him and he can get started on achieving that goal."

"All part of the master plan," I said.

"Well if I left everything to him he'd never get around

to asking me out."

Good point, she was probably right. Crystal's eyes widened and I felt drops of water on my back.

"Would you mind backing away a bit, Sean," I said as I turned around.

"You're sitting on my towel," he said, giving me an evil grin before shaking his head and spraying the two of us with water.

We jumped up and backed away from the spray.

"What did you say that scared Edwin away?" he asked as he grabbed the towel and started to dry off.

"What makes you think we said anything?" I asked.

Sean stopped and looked at me as if I was an idiot, an expression he'd taken with me quite a lot lately.

"You turned up and he left. It wasn't me that scared him off."

"He just needs to work some things out. Where's the girl Edwin said you were talking to?" I asked.

"Her boyfriend showed up," Sean said morosely.

I looked behind him and, sure enough, there was a teenage girl giggling inanely to something the musclebound guy with her was saying.

"Better luck next time," I said.

Chapter Six

Getting back to the apartment complex, we found Miss Betsy standing at the front, a worried look on her face.

"Thank goodness you're here," she said, twisting her hands together.

"What's wrong?" I asked.

"That policeman who has been to see you sometimes, he came and took Edwin away."

"He did what?" I exploded.

"He and that pretty woman who comes with him, they arrested Edwin and took him away," Miss Betsy repeated.

"Get back in the car, Crystal," I said as she started to get out.

"What about me?" asked Sean.

"You stay here with Miss Betsy, we'll find out what's happening with Edwin."

"What's going on?" asked a bewildered Crystal as I pulled out of the parking area.

"Griffin arrested Edwin."

"He did what?"

Oh, that didn't sound good. Crystal was going with her calm voice. Bad things had a tendency to happen when Crystal used her calm voice in an emotional situation. ·

"Call your lawyer and get him to meet us at the station," I said, desperately trying to head off an explosion.

Walking into the station, I refused to dwell on the number of times that I seemed to be finding myself in this particular building. At least this time I wasn't going to end up in the interrogation room, or at least I hoped not. Crystal stormed up to the front desk and caught the attention of the officer.

"I demand to see Detective Griffin," she announced and I winced.

I love Crystal but every now and then the spoiled Hollywood princess comes out in her. Those of us who are her friends deal with it and can laugh it off. I didn't think that the officer behind the desk was in a laughing mood. To his credit though, he restrained himself from telling Crystal exactly what she could do with her demand, and very politely asked her to take a seat while he fetched Griffin. He also called her ma'am repeatedly, after the first one elicited a tightening of her features. Couldn't really blame the guy for getting in his digs when he could. Sitting with Crystal in the waiting area was interesting. Being relatively early in the day, we were obviously not being treated to the full experience that only a police station at night can offer. As the time dragged on I could see that Crystal was beginning to lose her patience. As she started to get up again to harangue the poor desk sergeant, I put a hand on her arm.

"Not going to help," I said. I had noticed the smirk on the officer's face as he saw her movement.

Nope, Crystal hadn't made any friends there. The lawyer that Crystal had contacted came in and, after speaking with Crystal, was led into the back area to his client.

"What is taking so long?" she said through gritted teeth.

"I don't know," I said, looking anxiously towards the door.

"They've got the wrong person, Edwin could never hurt anyone."

"I know that, and you know that. Griffin will work that out. He's not an idiot and he'll work out that there is no way that Edwin could have done this."

"I need to get some air," said Crystal.

"I'll come with you." I started to stand up.

"No, I just need some time on my own to clear my

head. Can you wait here and let me know immediately if Edwin comes out."

"Of course," I said as I sat back down.

A few minutes later I started wondering whether I should have gone out with her. The door to the station flew open and half a dozen cops were struggling to drag in a well-dressed woman who was screaming and yelling abuse at the top of her lungs. I was surprised to see Travis Cooper, private investigator to the rich and famous, following her. Looking startled when he spotted me, he left the struggling cops and made his way over, taking a seat next to me.

"Interesting entrance," I motioned in the direction of the woman. "What happened there?"

"Client of mine, found out her husband was cheating on her with the housekeeper."

"Classy, if a bit unoriginal," I said.

"I only ever deal with the best," he smiled.

"Obviously there is another part to this story because she does not look like a satisfied client."

"Yes, she didn't take it too well and went after her husband with a set of gardening shears."

I grimaced at the image that crossed my mind.

"Luckily, or unluckily, whichever the case may be, I was there so was able to stop the impending bloodbath and called the cops."

"On your own client. Hope you weren't still expecting to get paid," I said.

"There's a reason why I always get paid up front. Won't be getting a bonus this time though."

I laughed at the morose look on his face.

"So what are you doing here, another client die mysteriously?"

"I have never lost a client," I said defensively.

"No, of course not, just the people around them start dropping like flies."

"I could be here to pay a parking fine."

"You're here to pay a parking fine." He looked at me skeptically.

"Well no, but I could be here for that reason. You shouldn't automatically assume someone's died just because I'm in a police station."

Travis continued to study me without saying a word.

"Fine, Catarina Badal was killed last night at a theater and I was at the after party. My friend Edwin is being questioned by Griffin at the moment."

"See, was that so hard?" Travis asked.

"You just can't assume that I'd be here because of a murder," I said, trying to get my point across.

"And yet that's exactly the reason why you're here."

"I don't like you very much," I said sullenly. "Don't you have a client to send to jail?"

"Oh, sweetheart, that hurts, got me right here," he said, pointing to his heart with a comical look on his face. I burst out laughing at the absurdity of the situation.

Travis glanced behind me. "I think we're in trouble," he said, a wide grin splitting his face.

I turned around and almost groaned when I looked into the more than slightly annoyed face of one Detective Jake Griffin. Luckily, I was saved from having to come up with anything to say because at that moment Crystal walked in and stormed up to Griffin.

"It's about time. Where is he and what have you done to him?"

"Miss Bronstein," he said. "Mr Litchfield is currently providing some samples to assist us with our inquiries. If you could please take a seat and show some patience, he will be out soon. However, if you choose not to take those options, we will be forced to remove you."

Tact and diplomacy, not really Griffin's strong points. The sergeant who had been subjected to Crystal when she first came in seemed to appreciate it though. He sat back in his chair, crossed his arms and enjoyed the show. Crystal opened her mouth and I braced myself waiting for what came next, but she obviously thought better of it and closed it again.

"Miss Eyre, could I speak to you please?"

And we were back to Miss Eyre. A woman could get whiplash trying to deal with the moods of a man like this.

"Looks like you're in trouble," Travis said in a low voice.

"Like that's new," I whispered back.

"See you around," he smiled.

I nodded and followed Griffin to the back, once again into an interrogation room. So much for thinking I wouldn't be ending up back in here. He closed the door and I turned to face him.

"So, did you want to tell me why you arrested my friend not long after coming to see me and…"

I waved my hand rather than talking about the session at my apartment.

"And what?" he asked.

"You know perfectly well what," I said.

"Yes, but I'd kind of be interested in hearing you say it."

"Despite what you may believe, I am not here for your entertainment," I said. "You know perfectly well that Edwin is not capable of murdering somebody."

"Actually, I don't know that. I don't know him at all. As far as I know at this stage it is something he is perfectly capable of doing. He was the last person to see Catarina alive so he had the opportunity. She'd just humiliated him so he had the motive. The knife was one that was in her office as a decoration so he had the means."

"Please tell me that isn't all you're basing your case on," I said.

Griffin looked at me sourly. "Of course it isn't, but I have to do my job and he is a viable suspect."

"Of course, your job," I said.

"Don't," Griffin growled.

"Don't what?"

"I am not going to let you use this to try to shove me away again. I will do my job because that is who I am, but you were right. Previously I've used you to get information for cases. I won't be doing that this time. In fact I don't want you anywhere near this case. When we are together we won't be discussing it at all."

"That's going to be a bit difficult when you arrested one of my closest friends."

"But that is how we are going to do it."

I looked at him inquiringly. "I don't know how it works for you but I'm really not the kind of person who can just sit around while my innocent friend gets accused of something he didn't do."

"Well this time that is exactly what you are going to do. You have walked into the middle of my cases twice already and both times you've almost got yourself killed. I'm not willing to take the chance of that happening again," Griffin said.

"You know, I love how you are making these sweeping statements as if you actually have a say in what I do."

"You get involved in this case and I'm going to arrest you for interfering in my investigation," Griffin's scowl deepened.

"I don't know where you get your dating advice from, but a little hint, threatening a woman with arrest is a really bad step in a courtship."

Griffin's mood changed instantly from annoyed to seducing. I could see the change come over him as his eyes took on a lazy warm look. He stepped closer to me and I stepped back hitting the door.

"Stop it," I said imperiously, putting both hands out in front of me. "We are not doing this up against another wall."

"Honey, I am all for getting horizontal with you if that's what you'd prefer."

He leaned in and gave me a soft feathery kiss against my neck, in that spot just below my ear which was

35

guaranteed to start me thinking very happy thoughts. I tilted my head slightly and he groaned.

"You have no idea how much I want to continue this," he said quietly, "but this is not the place and next time I get you in this position I want a lot of time and no chance of us being interrupted."

He gave me another kiss and stepped back, smiling wolfishly as he saw the glazed look on my face. It took me a couple of seconds to realize our moment was over and that once again he had quite successfully distracted me.

I looked at him seriously. "Edwin couldn't have done this. I know him and he is just not capable of doing something so terrible."

Griffin looked at me regretfully. "I know you believe that," he said, "and I wish I could take that into account, but I've been at this job a long time and everyone is capable of doing terrible things. I have to follow the evidence, wherever it leads. Please tell me you understand that."

I nodded. "I understand, but you are wrong and I won't be able to keep out of this if you insist on accusing Edwin. He didn't do this."

Griffin sighed. "I admire your loyalty to him but just keep in mind that people can disappoint you sometimes."

I nodded. "Are we done?"

"For now, but you need to remember that I want you to stay out of this."

I nodded again, it's easier to misinterpret a nod than it is a direct answer. In this case my nod meant that I knew he wanted me to stay out of this but I was still going to do what I thought was right. From the tightening of Griffin's face, I got the feeling that he knew exactly what my nod meant. Before he could try to talk me out of it I surprised him by giving him a quick kiss on the cheek.

"Bye," I said, turned around, opened the door and stepped out quickly.

Getting to the front desk I was in time to see Edwin

walk out. Crystal jumped up with a cry and threw herself at him. Edwin wrapped his arms around her and started stroking her back as he murmured into her ear. I stopped and let them have their moment. If any good was coming out of this situation, it was that two people who meant a lot to me were finally working out that they meant the world to each other.

"You guys ready to go?" I asked.

Crystal turned to me, surreptitiously wiping her eyes. "I think so."

I looked inquiringly at Edwin.

"I'm done," he said curtly, his eyes drifting past me and I knew that Griffin had followed me out.

"See you later, Travis," I said as I hustled the two of them out.

He grinned. "With your track record, I'm betting I'll see you soon."

I grimaced. "Just be careful of your next client."

Travis's booming laughter followed us out of the station.

Chapter Seven

By mutual agreement the three of us ended up in my apartment, breaking open a tub of ice cream.

"So," said Crystal, breaking the silence. "Were you planning on telling us exactly why the cops think you killed the director?"

Edwin studied the tub intently.

"Edwin," I said gently. "We need to know if we are going to help you."

Edwin dropped his spoon and looked away.

"The cops think that I killed her because she said some things about my acting. They think I killed her in a fit of wounded pride and rage."

"Why would they think that?" Crystal asked as she scooped up some ice cream. "Catarina had a go at everyone. What makes you so special?"

Edwin looked discomfited. "Yes, but I was the idiot who slept with her."

Crystal stopped eating and stared at him. Deliberately, she put her spoon down and got up off the floor where we had made ourselves comfortable. Without looking at us she left the room and I heard the front door open and close. Edwin's head dropped back against the couch cushion.

"I didn't want to tell her."

"I can understand why." I shook my head. "What were you thinking, sleeping with her?"

Edwin shrugged his shoulders. "It was one time. I don't know why I did it. She was there and she was willing. She kept telling me that she could see a great actor in me. I know now it was all just a load of garbage, but at the time I was feeling pretty low. Believe me, I knew it was a mistake straight away. Do you think Crystal will forgive me?"

"Of course she will," I said, squeezing his hand. "It just might take a bit of time for her to get her head around it."

Of course it would be a period of time when she was going to make Edwin miserable.

"So, is that the only reason the cops are looking at you for the murder, the fact that you slept with her?"

Edwin nodded.

"How did the cops find out about it, if it only happened the once."

Edwin refused to look me in the eye.

"Seems she kept a diary which listed all the men she slept with and had comments and a rating system."

"That's disturbing," I said.

I looked at him and when he looked back, I quickly glanced away.

Edwin sighed. "No, they didn't tell me what my rating was or what she wrote about me."

"I wasn't going to ask," I protested, and Edwin raised an eyebrow at me. "They must have other suspects then if she kept a diary of all her..." my voice tapered off.

"Conquests," Edwin supplied dryly.

"I was going to say partners," I said defensively.

"Because that makes it sound so much better," Edwin said sarcastically.

"Do you want an argument with me?" I said, starting to get annoyed.

Edwin dropped his head back again. "No, I'm just mad at myself for being so stupid. I've had a thing for Crystal for so long but I've always just been in the friend zone. I guess I got to the point where I figured that was all I'd ever be. Between thinking she could never be interested in me and realizing that I was never going to make it as an actor, I started doing some pretty stupid things and this was just one of them."

I hated hearing him sound so defeated, it just didn't sound like the optimistic Edwin that I usually talked to.

"So, what are you going to do about it?" I asked.

"What do you mean?" Edwin looked perplexed.

"I mean, how about you suck it up and deal with the situation in front of you."

Edwin's phone chose that moment to ring. He held it up and waved it in front of me. "Saved by the proverbial bell."

I smiled cheerlessly and went back to eating my ice cream. After his call finished, I looked at him expectantly.

"That was Catarina's assistant, seems like the funeral is being held tomorrow."

"Already?" I queried. "Don't the police still have the body for examination?"

"I don't know, all I know is that the funeral is tomorrow. Catarina's assistant, Peter, is planning it and he's trying to get as many people there as he can."

"Even though you're a suspect," I said slowly.

Edwin shrugged. "I said it might not be appropriate that I be there, but I've worked with him and he insisted he knows the police have it wrong and that I should have the opportunity to grieve for Catarina like everyone else."

I know I looked skeptical.

"He's been with Catarina for years and from what I saw is pretty devoted to her. He probably truly believes there will be people grieving for her."

"Do you want company?" I asked.

Edwin's gratitude was palpable. "Thank you, yes. I really don't want to turn up to that thing on my own, especially if people are thinking that I could have killed her."

After Edwin left I went to Crystal's apartment and, using my emergency key for a change, I opened the door. Sure enough, she was in her room burrowed under the covers. Grabbing hold of one end I gave it a yank to find her curled up with streaks of tears down her face. Hardening myself to her obvious distress, I put my hands on my hips.

"I didn't really think that hiding was your style."

Crystal waved her hands around while gulping in air. I waited until she could talk.

"He slept with her, I love him and he slept with her."

I sat down on the bed.

"Have you told him you love him?"

Crystal paused and then shook her head.

"Didn't you go out on a date just a couple of nights ago with that artist freak who wanted to pose you with post it notes covering your body and use you for his latest showing?"

"Well, yes," she said.

"So maybe having a go at Edwin over something he did before you started showing all this interest in him is a little unfair."

Crystal glared at me mutinously. "Number one, you are ignoring your role as best friend. Regardless of how stupid my feelings are at this point I don't want logic. I want you to provide chocolate and agree with me that he did the wrong thing. I'd do it for you."

"I know you would, and with any other guy I would be right there with you. But this is Edwin, who you have been in love with for ages. Despite the fact you date like it's a competition and whoever has the highest number wins. If you play this wrong, you could lose him and I know you don't want that."

Crystal tossed her pillow at me halfheartedly.

"I know, I just… I've never been jealous, not with any guy I've been out with and here I am hating a dead woman because he slept with her."

"Well," I said, standing up, "you'll need to get over it, because tomorrow you and I are going to accompany Edwin to her funeral. We are going to be appropriately respectful and somber and we will support our friend. Are we clear?"

"Yes, Mom," she said with a glint in her eye.

I sighed. "Now why would you go and insult me like that?"

Crystal grimaced. "Sorry, you're really nothing like my mom."

After the many stories Crystal had told me of her mother and her many maternal failings, I would hope not.

Chapter Eight

The next morning, as the three of us entered the funeral home, I was surprised at the small number of people there. Catarina's assistant, Peter, greeted us.

"Thank you so much for coming." His eyes were shiny with unshed tears as he clasped Edwin's hands. His eyes widened as he saw Crystal. In Hollywood, Crystal's father is considered someone who can make and break careers. In the social set she is considered pure gold, so the fact that she had turned up for Catarina's funeral meant something. The fact she was there for Edwin and not for Catarina didn't come into it. She was there so that upped the social tone of the funeral. It was all about appearances, even when you were dead.

Looking around though, it would seem that appearances weren't exactly working for Catarina. There were a few of the actors that I remembered from the play she had been directing. Sure enough, in the back of the room, keeping their eyes on everyone attending, were Detectives Griffin and Ramos. Feeling a little unsure of myself, I briefly nodded in their direction and looked away. I shouldn't have been surprised to see Tomas Burnelli attending. Tomas used to work as a personal assistant for Monique, like I did. However, he had found his calling as a funeral events planner. I wasn't surprised to see that he was here. I'd used him myself when having to organize a funeral, and he was very good at pulling together a tasteful send off for the dearly departed in a very short period of time. Seeing me, Tomas's eyes lit up and he headed in my direction.

"Trudie, my dear," he said in that voice of his which managed to be both quiet and respectful, but with a hint of the party personality he had to keep hidden while working. I could tell it just wanted to burst through though.

"I haven't heard from you in months, but I did see that photo online of you and Kai Roth."

I dropped my head and had to stop myself from groaning. During my last job with the teenage prodigy from hell I committed the cardinal sin of an assistant and got noticed. One night I had to drag the most gifted singer of the current generation (his words, not mine), drunk out of his mind, away from a strip club. Unfortunately, his brain had not caught up with the fact that the woman he was trying to maul was not one of the delightful strippers in the club who had been, oh so friendly, when he started throwing the cash around, but his perfectly boring assistant. Unfortunately for me, during this time when I was trying to fend off the dozen hands he seemed to have grown, a couple of paparazzi, showing their usual exquisite timing, had taken a photo. The next day, the headline had screamed about the teenage singer and his new cougar girlfriend.

At twenty-five years of age I was a cougar. Ever been the focus of a teenage girl hate campaign? I've seen sharks in a feeding frenzy more friendly that those girls were. Social media lit up and I was enemy number one on the teenage girl hit list. I have never been called an old, ugly slut in so many descriptive ways in my life. Of course, the little, let's use the term pop star for now, refused to clarify the situation. He just let it go, feeding on the collective outrage. Another reason I was really glad that job was over. That and the excruciatingly uncomfortable conversation I had with my grandmother, who tried to gently suggest that he might be a little too young and too wild for me.

"Is this one of your cases?" Tomas whispered conspiratorially.

"No." I lowered my voice to match his. "A friend of mine worked with her and I'm just here with him."

"So disappointing." Tomas shook his head.

The last time I was involved with a funeral that Tomas organized, a second wife turned up and disrupted proceedings quite spectacularly. Obviously Tomas looked at that event not so much as a failed funeral, but as a piece of soap opera like entertainment. Looking back on it, I had to agree.

"Your delicious policeman is here," Tomas whispered.

"He's not my delicious policeman," I said automatically.

"Honey, the way that man looks at you, believe me he is your delicious policeman. You just need to be brave enough to take a bite."

That threw up a few interesting images. I looked up and sure enough Griffin was staring at me with an expression that could only be described as hot and possessive. For the first time, that thought didn't fill me with panic. I smiled to myself. Maybe I was getting used to this.

"Have you been in to see Catarina yet?"

"No, not yet," I said. "I'm pretty sure I don't want to see her."

"Oh, you have to see her. Helena really did a fabulous job today," Tomas said excitedly.

Helena was a funeral cosmetologist who prepared bodies for viewing. She was a little unusual in the way she approached her profession, but she had an amazing talent. Tomas dragged me into the viewing area so I could have the opportunity to see Helena's latest miracle. Reluctantly peering into the coffin, I gasped.

"She looks amazing. Seriously, she didn't look this good last time I saw her. I swear, Helena's taken ten years off the woman."

Tomas smiled happily. It was good to know someone who took so much pride in their work. Looking down at her, I noticed a small photo held in her hands where they were crossed over her heart. I looked closer.

"Is that a cat?" I asked.

Tomas nodded. "Yes, it was a special request. According to Peter, her assistant, Catarina loved that cat more than anyone."

I could understand that. From the little I'd seen of Catarina Badal, human relationships had not exactly been her strong point. At that moment Peter came rushing in with a cat carrier. I could hear what sounded like growling and hissing emanating from the cage. Peter himself didn't look great either. He had scratches on his hands and red patches on his face.

"Oh my God," I said. "Are you alright?"

Peter sniffed while he placed the cat cage next to the coffin. Hunting in his pocket he drew out a wadded up tissue.

"I'm fine," he said. "Catarina would have wanted Cleopatra here. Excuse me."

Turning his head, he blew his nose, long and loud. I could see an angry red rash building on the back of his neck.

"Seriously, Peter," I said. "Do you need to see someone? You're not looking very well."

Peter sniffed again as he tucked the tissues back in his pocket. "I'm okay, I just have a couple of small allergies to cats."

I looked at him doubtfully. His left eye seemed to be swelling shut.

"Maybe you should go to the restroom and tidy yourself up a bit," I suggested gently. "We'll take care of the cat for you if you want."

Peter blinked up at me. His left eye was starting to water and the red rashes on his face seemed to be getting angrier.

"You're right of course," he said, blinking rapidly. "Thank you, but you can't leave Cleopatra," he said.

"Not for an instant," I promised and Tomas nodded beside me.

After watching Peter leave, I turned to Tomas and we both hunkered down and looked at the cat through the front of the cat cage. Cleopatra looked unremarkable, if you didn't take into account that she made a noise that sounded like an out of tune violin interspersed with hissing and her tail lashing.

"Doesn't look happy," I said.

"Should we take it out?" suggested Tomas. "So it can say goodbye."

"Did you see Peter's hands?" I said. "There is no way that I am going anywhere near that cat."

Tomas looked down at his perfectly manicured hands and shrugged. Decision obviously made, he straightened up.

"I have some last minute items to take care of," he said. "Can you stay with the cat until Peter comes back?"

"Sure," I said. When he left I realized that I had volunteered to stay in a room with a corpse and a very angry cat. Faced with a decision between talking to the dead woman or to the cat, I chose the less creepy of the two options.

"So," I said, "I'm guessing you're a little bit confused right now." The cat glared at me balefully and started up that growling noise which was quickly reaching a screech.

"It's okay, sweetie," I crooned soothingly. "We'll get you through this and then I'm sure there's going to be something very nice for you to eat at the end of it."

The cat started to quieten at the thought of food.

"That's right." I worked my fingers between the bars of the cage in a vain attempt to stroke the calming cat, and just barely pulled back in time as the cat let out her claws and took a swipe.

"What the hell are you doing?" I spun around and there was Griffin standing behind me, hands on hips with a quizzical look on his face.

"Cat, Catarina's cat. Peter asked me to keep an eye on it."

I stopped as I noticed that Griffin was trying manfully to suppress a smile.

"One of these days you're going to have to tell me how you end up in these situations," he said, shaking his head.

"A pathological inability to say no," I replied.

"Really?" queried Griffin. "You don't seem to have a problem with saying no to me."

"You're different," I said.

"Good," Griffin replied.

"What do you mean, good?" I asked, a little irritated.

"Different means I'm special, different means you can't walk away and forget about me."

I cleared my throat. "Are we having a moment? Because if we are, I think you're forgetting about the dead woman and her psychotic cat."

Griffin sighed.

"Yeah, I know. One of these days we're actually going to have to go on a date that doesn't involve a dead body."

"You are such a romantic," I said, smiling.

"Trudie, are you in here?"

Griffin and I turned to see Crystal and Edwin tentatively entering the room. Seeing Griffin with me, their reactions were quite different. Edwin went pale and Crystal went red. Kind of described their two personalities in a nutshell really. Thankfully, and rather surprisingly, Crystal chose to remain quiet. Maybe the woman was learning self-control. After an uncomfortable silence Griffin cleared his throat.

"I'll speak to you later, Trudie," he said.

"Wouldn't want to get in the way of you accusing other innocent people of murder," Crystal piped in.

I dropped my head. Looked like I spoke too soon. Ignoring Crystal completely, Griffin left the room.

"Did you really have to do that?" I asked Crystal.

Defiantly, Crystal flipped her hair back.

"He deserves it, if he put half as much attention into actually finding the murderer as he has done hassling poor

Edwin, the whole case would be closed and we wouldn't be in here with a…what is a cat doing in here?"

"It's Catarina's cat, her assistant felt it should be here for the funeral."

Crystal looked at me strangely.

"Cats are important to some people."

Crystal turned on Edwin.

"This is what happens when you use your little brain and not your big one, you sleep with the crazy cat lady."

Turning around, she stalked out of the room.

"Why is she being so nuts over this?" Edwin asked with a plaintive tone in his voice. "She's never even thought about who I slept with before and it was just the one time with Catarina. It's not like it meant anything."

"Number one, the woman is lying there, dead. I really don't think this is the place for this conversation. Number two, maybe the situation has changed recently and you should start adapting to the new regime," I said.

Edwin looked confused and I didn't really feel like enlightening him any further. I learned long ago to avoid getting entangled in other people's love lives, especially friends. Things have a tendency to get messy when you step in the middle of those situations. Edwin looked over at Catarina and his face softened.

"Sometimes life happens so quickly, one minute you're there and the next you're gone," he said.

I put an arm around his shoulder. "And that is why we live the best life we can, we appreciate what we have and we tell the people we love, that we love them."

"Wise words indeed," said a voice from behind us.

Edwin and I turned around and found an older man looking at Catarina's body. He looked to be in his late forties, his dark brown hair showing streaks of gray.

"You would do well to listen to your friend," he directed at Edwin. "Life just goes too fast and before you know it, you look back and see it cluttered with regrets."

He looked at Catarina again and I was surprised to see

an expression of bitterness on his face.

"My name is Trudie and this is Edwin."

Still looking at Catarina he nodded. "I'm Evan Webber, I'm Catarina's husband."

I felt as much as heard Edwin's quick intake of breath.

"I'll go find Crystal," he muttered, before quickly making his exit.

Evan's eyes followed him out of the room and then he looked at me thoughtfully.

"Your young man slept with my wife didn't he?"

"He's not my young man," I said, desperately trying not to answer the question.

"It doesn't matter," the older man said. "It's not like Catarina and I had much of a marriage left anyway."

"I'm sorry," I said, raising my voice as if it was a question.

"So was I, so many times," he sighed. "I was her English professor in college. When I think of it now I should have realized something wasn't right. She was so beautiful and full of life, and she wanted me." He frowned. "I was never the type to catch the attention of a woman like her."

I didn't know what to say. Catarina had the looks and personality that were larger than life, and Evan was right. He looked exactly like what he was, a conservative English professor.

"I had one thing that she wanted though," he continued on. "I had the social group that she was interested in, that she knew could help her career. I was a networking tool for her. She always got what she wanted and if you got in the way she would walk right over you. She knew what she wanted the first day she walked into my classroom and I made it easy for her."

I stayed silent. He seemed to be lost in his memories and it was like he had forgotten that I was even there.

"I was so besotted with her, I would have done anything that she wanted. I supported everything she did.

No matter what she did, I was there for her, through the alcohol, the gambling, the other men."

He shook his head.

"I stood by you, didn't I?" he directed at the dead woman. "And when I said I wanted a divorce, you wouldn't give me one because that would have meant parting with some of the money you'd earned climbing over the top of everyone. Looks like I'm finally free at last," he whispered, tears shimmering in his eyes.

At this point I wasn't entirely sure whether those tears were from grief or joy. Feeling extraordinarily uncomfortable, I almost wept with joy when Peter arrived, looking slightly less inflamed than he had earlier. The cat, who had stayed blissfully quiet, took one look at Peter and started yowling again. I could hear the tail swishing against the sides of the cage. Peter slowed as he saw who else was next to the coffin.

"Evan," he said. "I didn't expect you to be here."

"Why not?" Evan replied. "She was my wife after all."

"Only in name," said Peter.

Evan inclined his head in acknowledgment of the truth of that statement.

"It was lovely to meet you, Trudie. Thank you for listening to the sentimental ramblings of an old fool."

I watched him leave, noticing that he seemed to be holding himself a little straighter as if a burden had been lifted from him.

"He's right," Peter mumbled as he went to grab the cat cage. "He always was an old fool, even when he was younger. He couldn't see that he never had a chance of holding on to Catarina."

"Why didn't they just divorce?" I asked.

"Catarina didn't want to lose any of her money to him in a divorce. Being married to him didn't make one tiny bit of difference to the way she lived her life so she just refused to divorce him. It probably gave her some perverse kind of enjoyment to know that he was trapped. Last I heard he had started seeing another professor at the university and wanted to marry her. Catarina liked the idea of standing in the way of his happily ever after, purely because she could."

I looked back at the coffin with a sense of distaste. Peter followed my look and his features tightened.

"She wasn't always like that," he said tightly.

"Of course not," I said. See, I was learning how to lie like the best of them.

Chapter Nine

Catarina's funeral was unlike any funeral service I had ever seen. The crowd was small but there was not one tear from anyone that I could see. The eulogy was given in the same way that a stock report would be given, just a litany of the highlights. Admittedly, from what I'd heard about Catarina's personality, I wasn't really surprised but I had thought that there must be someone who would mourn her passing. Someone other than the cat who spent the entire service in her cage, growling and hissing, providing a surreal backdrop to the extremely uncomfortable situation.

Later, standing in a corner during the wake with Crystal and Edwin, I looked around the subdued group again. At the wakes I had been to previously, there would be any number of emotions on show, from devastation to a bleak humor, as people discussed their memories of the dearly departed. Today, there seemed to be nothing. I could see poor Tomas had no idea what to do with himself. It was like a party where no one had any clue why they were there, and were trying to work out how much time they had to stay before they could make their escape without seeming to be rude.

"This is starting to creep me out," Crystal murmured.

"Got that right," a voice came from behind me and I spun around to find Travis Cooper standing there with a grin on his face and holding a huge plate of food.

"What are you doing here?" I asked, possibly not as surprised as I should have been. The man seemed to pop up in the strangest places.

Travis shrugged and that crooked smile of his started to show.

"I came to be your date."

I rolled my eyes, holding back a sigh. "People don't bring dates to funerals."

"The husband did." Travis motioned to where Evan Webber was standing next to an older woman, his head bent to hers as if unwilling to miss a single word that she said.

"You are kidding me," Crystal said, unable to stop herself from looking in the direction he was pointing.

"Afraid not," said Travis, a little too gleefully.

The man seemed to get a perverse pleasure from seeing the all too human foibles on show. Despite the fact I wouldn't put it past him to be here purely for the entertainment value, I felt my eyes narrowing at him.

"Were you planning on telling us the real reason why you are here or did you want us to play twenty questions so you can be entertained?"

"See, that's why we're perfect for each other," Travis said. "You understand me."

I had to stop myself from rolling my eyes. We weren't perfect for each other. Travis just had a complicated history with Griffin that I knew part of but not all. Somehow I had become this bone of contention between them. Travis seemed to enjoy pushing Griffin's buttons by being around me and behaving slightly inappropriately. I didn't take him seriously, but unfortunately Griffin still reacted badly when Travis came anywhere near me. Fortunately, he and Ramos had left the funeral after the service, thereby missing the most lackluster wake ever.

"I'm actually working today."

"Ooh," said Crystal, scanning the crowd. "Who's the dirty cheater? It's him isn't it?" she said, pointing to a possible aspiring actor who was obviously looking at character parts as a mob enforcer. His shirt was unbuttoned just a little too much, with gold chains showing on his extraordinarily hairy chest. He was speaking intently to Peter who was holding the cat cage in front of him as if it was a shield. Travis's hand shot out and clamped over Crystal's arm, pulling it down.

"No it isn't," he hissed, "and it might not be a great idea to bring attention to one of the more vicious debt collectors in the country."

"Really, what would he be doing at Catarina's funeral?" I asked quizzically as the three of us turned to look at him.

"Seriously, people," Travis said. "Stop looking at him. Believe me, he is a man you do not want to get the attention of."

We turned back to him.

"I'm actually here for the husband."

"Why would you be looking into the husband? Who's he cheating on?"

Travis looked at me sourly. "You know, I don't just take on cheating jobs. I do have other skills."

"Of course you do," I said, hoping I was conveying my sincerity appropriately.

Travis looked at me in disgust. "As we know, Catarina and Evan's marriage was not a happy one, both pretty much divorced except for the paperwork. Evan started seeing a professor from college, much more his speed. He's trying to convince Catarina to give him a divorce so he can marry the academic of his dreams. Catarina refuses and now Catarina is dead. Evan can now marry the woman he loves, no harm, no foul. Problem though is that Catarina was removed from the picture in a pretty unsavory way. The professor has got a daughter who, understandably, is a bit concerned that the wife of her future stepfather was dispatched in such a way. I have been hired to look into the case to ensure that mom is safe with her prince charming."

"Really?" I was having a little trouble stopping the skepticism from showing. I knew Travis's reputation and I also knew that he was not cheap. The thought that someone had hired him for this kind of job didn't quite sound right. Usually people hired him when there was a chance of a major pay off.

Travis sighed. "That was the reason I got given but I looked into it. The professor over there has money and I'm guessing the real reason is the daughter doesn't want anything to get in the way of her inheritance, a new husband may do that."

That sounded more like it.

"So what have you found so far?" asked Crystal excitedly.

"That if I was married to Catarina Badal I'd have killed her way before now," Travis said.

"How much exactly do they pay you for your brilliant insights?" I asked dryly.

"Not as much as I'm worth, sweetheart." Travis grinned.

"So, do you think he killed her?"

Travis shrugged, "He had every reason to. She seduced him, forced him into marriage with a fake pregnancy scare, used him to further her career and then refused to let him go when he fell for someone else, and believe me, from what I've found out he has definitely fallen for the other woman."

"Enough to kill?" I asked.

Travis shrugged. "And there is the million dollar question isn't it? I haven't found anything to indicate that he did kill her, but it's still a possibility. The fact of the matter is that he is now free to marry the new girlfriend and we haven't even looked at what he could be getting out of the will." We all looked thoughtfully over at Evan as he precariously juggled a plate and a drink, all while listening solicitously to his soon to be wife, if what Travis was telling us was true.

"I really think we should go," announced Crystal.

"Over it already?" I asked.

"I was over it before we walked in the door," she said.

"No problems," I said. "Just give me few minutes to find Tomas and say goodbye."

"You're just going to leave me here," Travis whined

plaintively.

"Afraid so," I said. "Maybe you'll get lucky and he'll be overcome with guilt and admit to killing her."

Travis looked at me sourly. "You know, sometimes I really don't think that you take me seriously."

Looking for Tomas, I rounded a corner to see the man Travis had said was the debt collector with Peter, cornered in the hallway. Peter looked panicked.

"Your boss stole from Mr Caldwell and owed him a lot of money."

"But she's dead," sputtered Peter.

"You really think that matters to Mr Caldwell," he drawled. "That money needs to be paid sooner or later by someone. If it isn't her then those close to her need to start coming up with the cash."

A hand touched my arm and I leapt back clapping a hand over my mouth to stifle the scream that was coming out.

"What are you...?" Tomas managed to get out before I clapped the other hand over his mouth. The debt collector looked in our direction and, seeing a door behind us, I opened it and quickly pulled Tomas in, still with my hand clamped over his mouth. In the darkness I could see that I had pulled us into a closet. Tomas, obviously knowing that there must be a reason for my crazy antics, didn't struggle and stood there patiently with my hand covering his mouth. I could hear footsteps coming down the hall. Through the light coming underneath the doorway I could see a shadow as a figure stopped. I held my breath and I could feel that Tomas had stopped breathing against me hand. Neither of us moved as we both looked at the doorknob, willing it not to turn.

"Because I'm a generous man, I'm giving you one chance to make this right. If not, you just may be looking at joining your boss."

Tomas's eyes widened and we listened as heavy footsteps made their way down the hall. Lighter ones went in the opposite direction and I started to breathe again. Just as my racing heart started to calm down, the door was pulled open. I gave a short scream that got strangled when I saw it was Travis standing in the doorway. He looked at the two of us standing in the closet, my hand still covering Tomas's mouth and leaned back.

"Not what I was expecting to find, but hell, I've seen worse."

I dropped my hand. "You've probably been part of worse," I hissed.

Travis shrugged. "Not going to argue with you there."

"What are you doing here?" I asked as I came out of the closet, peering around to make sure we were alone.

"Crystal and Edwin got into an argument over some stupid thing. Crystal stormed out and Edwin went after her. I told him I'd take you home."

"What were they arguing about?" I asked.

"I don't know," he said impatiently. "It just seemed like some weird kind of foreplay they were doing. Frankly, the whole thing made me uncomfortable."

"I would have thought it would take a lot to make you uncomfortable."

"Exactly," he replied. "Gives you an idea of how bad it was."

"So you came looking for me. How did you know I was in the closet?"

"Saw you drag the poor guy in here. I was just getting ready to rescue him when I saw D'Angelo. Figured I'd better get out of the way. When he was gone I came to get you."

"Did you see what happened?" I asked

"No, think I was too late, but anything that has D'Angelo involved is very bad news."

"He may have something to do with Catarina's death."

"Not a big leap," Travis said thoughtfully. "The guy works as a freelance debt collector for some of the casino owners in Vegas. Mostly works with the high rollers who have got in over their heads and think their position or their money means they don't have to pay. D'Angelo is very good at disabusing them of that notion. Looks like Catarina may have got herself in some trouble."

"Question is, could that have been the cause of her death?"

I noticed Tomas still standing there, not saying a word and with the same stunned look on his face that he had when I'd pulled him into the closet.

"Are you okay, Tomas?" I asked, the concern that I had traumatized him evident in my voice. "I'm sorry I did that, I was just scared we'd get caught."

"Are you kidding?" said Tomas. "That was amazing. I love it when you come to a funeral, it makes for the most exciting day."

Travis raised his eyebrows.

"Okay," I drew out slowly. "I think it's time that I got going. Wouldn't want your day to get too exciting. You ready to take me home?" I said to Travis.

He nodded and I started to follow him.

Down the hallway I whispered to Travis, "Is he still looking at me?"

Travis looked back. "Yes he is, I think he looks like he's in love."

I snorted. "I think I've just been a little unlucky with the funerals I've attended."

This time Travis snorted. "Sure, it's all about luck. Got nothing to do with you."

I got into his car and turned on him.

"What do you mean by that?"

"I'm just saying, you're one of those people that attract trouble wherever you go. Luck's got nothing to do with it."

"I do not attract trouble," I said. "I work in an industry which is highly volatile."

Travis laughed so hard that I could see tears coming out of his eyes.

"You're a personal assistant," he said. "It's not like you're working in counter intelligence. Just accept it. There are some people in this world who, when things hit the fan, they are standing right in the middle of it as it rains down on them. You, my friend, are one of those people."

"I truly don't like you very much," I said through gritted teeth.

"I know you say that, but I don't believe you," Travis said, smiling.

"You really should," I said warningly.

"Hey," he protested. "I'm not saying it's a bad thing. I like being around you when it comes raining down, the results are kind of entertaining."

I sighed. There really was no arguing with that.

Chapter Ten

Waving as Travis pulled out of the parking lot after he dropped me off, I found Miss Betsy working in the garden as I usually did. She straightened as she watched Travis drive off.

"A new young man for you?" she asked expectantly.

"No, not for me," I said.

"Why ever not?" Miss Betsy said as she brushed the dirt from her pants. "You're a sweet girl and deserve a good man."

"Then that definitely rules out Travis," I said, smiling.

Miss Betsy smiled back. "Sometimes the bad ones are the best kind," she said softly. "Although, I probably shouldn't be saying anything or that handsome police officer of yours might be a little unhappy with me."

I gave her a tight smile and she looked at me knowingly.

"So, the boy has made some progress has he?"

"What do you mean?" I asked.

"Well, this is the first time I've heard you not argue the point when someone has put the two of you together."

"He's growing on me."

"Persistent," she said. "That's good. I don't think your walls would have come down for anyone less than that."

I sat on the low garden wall. "What do you mean?"

Miss Betsy sat down next to me. "Your ex gave up on you when you needed him most, didn't he?"

I nodded slowly. Well, it was the truth. My ex-fiancé had walked into the hospital room where I was laying after a drunk driver decided to try to turn me into a hood ornament, and told me he didn't love me enough to be my caregiver if my injuries were permanent.

Miss Betsy continued when she saw my darkening

expression. "That kind of low act from the man you loved, no matter how strong you are, it's going to leave a scar. Makes it hard for you to trust another man. Any man who wants that trust is going to have to work for it, and work hard. The cop has made some mistakes."

I snorted indelicately.

"God knows the man looks fine but he's not overly smooth with the ladies, is he?" she asked.

I had to agree.

"But then you don't want smooth do you? You want strong and loyal, and from the looks of it, that cop has got those qualities in spades."

"So you think I should take a chance with him?" I asked tentatively.

"Honey, I am the last person in the world to tell you what man to take a chance on. My abilities at reading a good man from a bad one verge on the nonexistent. I have made so many mistakes in my life when it came to men, I should have given up on it years ago. What I will say, is that sometimes you let the right one go for all the wrong reasons. Don't let the one who betrayed you be the one who dictates how you live your life from now on. Learn from him but don't let him run your life."

"You're a very smart woman," I said.

"Not so smart," she said, smiling softly but with a touch of sadness flickering through her eyes. "If I had been smart I would have learned that lesson myself a long time ago and I would have been living the lesson not just doling out advice now."

I put my hand on the back of hers and squeezed it.

"If you ever need to talk about it, I'm right here, you know that. don't you?"

She turned over her hand and squeezed mine back.

"You are a sweet girl, letting an old woman ramble on like that, but some things are best left in the past."

I nodded and stood up.

"I'd better go find Crystal and Edwin, and find out

what happened to them. They ditched me at a funeral."

Miss Betsy shook her head, "I wouldn't go looking for them at the moment," she said. "They were arguing pretty bad when they got here earlier."

"Maybe I can help," I said.

"Oh, honey, the argument they were having is not one you can help with. I've had arguments like that before and, believe me, they end in one place. Trust me when I tell you that they are not going to want to be disturbed for a while."

"But, why, oh…" I said as her meaning finally became clear to me.

Miss Betsy nodded. "Yes, I would say they are at the making up portion of the proceedings. I personally would suggest keeping well away from the two of them for a while."

Good enough for me.

Chapter Eleven

As I walked up the stairs my cell phone rang. Answering it, I smiled when I heard Monique's rich voice. Struggling with my lock, I walked into my apartment.

"Hi Monique, what can I do for you?"

"You can tell me why it is that one of my favorite recruits was at the scene of a murder, again, and I didn't hear it directly from her."

I winced. Her voice was too calm, that never boded well.

"I was nowhere near the murder when it happened. I had a very peripheral part in this one, was barely even there."

"Oh, that's good," Monique said, although her voice still had a tone. "From what I heard, you discovered the body, got interviewed by the cops, your friend is a prime suspect and you attended the funeral."

Oh, so that was the reason for the tone. "See, peripheral, really, just on the edges," I said.

The silence coming down the phone was deafening. I could almost feel the disapproval beating at me but I was going to be strong, I wasn't going to cave.

"Okay, you're right, I should have called. I'm sorry."

Monique changed her tone. "Of course you should have called. I love you, darling. The thought of you going through such a traumatic event, it tears at me and then to know you didn't feel you could come to me with it, it breaks my heart."

Emotional guilt from Monique was always done so well.

"How did you hear about it anyway?" I asked

suspiciously.

"I have my sources," she said smoothly.

"Uh huh." Of course she had her sources. Nothing happened in this town without Monique knowing about it. If the woman ever decided to sell out to the tabloids, there would be mass panic in the streets. After twenty years networking in the background in Hollywood, Monique had information about everyone. Her staff had worked in every section of Hollywood and she learned and retained every piece of information she could find.

"So," said Monique. "I know you said you wanted some time off after the Kai Roth incident, but I've got a job that just came up for this afternoon and tonight. Should be an easy one."

I grunted. "That's what you said about the last job."

"Well, you had to know that I was lying on that one. I mean, for goodness sake, it was Kai Roth. That was never going to be pleasant. Anyway, you were desperate to get out of town. You would have taken that job no matter what I said."

I had to agree with her there. I knew walking into that job that I was dealing with the perceived stereotype of a spoiled pop star. Thanks to the internet, the whole world knew what Kai Roth was like.

"So why do you have a job for just one day?" I asked curiously.

"Blythe Stanton broke out of rehab for a club opening tonight. She's flying in from Europe right now. Her parents contacted me and they want someone to meet her at the airport and escort her until she leaves again tonight. She has a ticket to fly back to England at five tomorrow and it will be your job to make sure she is on that flight."

I sat down heavily. This was a babysitting job. Blythe Stanton was almost thirty years old and the heiress to a fortune in Europe. In her life she had dabbled as a singer and actress. She had been married and divorced three times already and was very well known to have a massive drug problem. Rumor had it that her father had finally got tired of her antics and told her that unless she did rehab and kicked the drugs, he was going to pull the trust fund which he still had complete control over. According to the tabloids she had gone into rehab in Switzerland. Sounded like the rehab hadn't really worked for her if she was making a break for it.

"Why on Earth is she coming here?" I asked.

"Seems one of the ex-husbands is opening a club in LA and she wants to be here for that. Whether it's to help him or destroy him is anyone's guess right now."

"She's a grown woman, Monique. How am I supposed to get her on that plane if she really doesn't want to go?" I asked.

"I'm going to be honest with you, Trudie, if you can't get her on the plane her parents are going to give up on her. The trust fund is going to be yanked, she'll be on her own. If you can impress that on her the best way you can, there isn't a lot else you can do."

"What about the drugs? If she wants to score I'll do the best I can to stop it but her reputation is well known. The second she hits the airport, word's going to go out and every dealer is going to hone in on us." I'd been through this kind of situation many times before.

"You're not going to have to deal with this on your own. I've sent in Jorge with you to help with security."

I started to breathe a little easier. Usually I don't have much time for security people of the rich and famous. I've had a few too many clashes with guys who are little more than thugs. Jorge was one of Monique's staff and there was a good reason for that. He was huge, with muscles on muscles and I had actually seen him move a car once by pushing it out of the way. The difference with other bodyguards was that he was also smart. If there was a way out of a situation without violence, he would take it.

"Okay, what time do I need to be at the airport for pick up?" I asked. I heard a knock at the door and dropped my head. "That's Jorge now, isn't it?" I asked Monique.

"Why, yes it is. That man does have an exquisite sense of timing."

I opened the door and, sure enough, there was Jorge in a tight t-shirt that left absolutely nothing to the imagination. His tattooed arms bulged out of the sleeves and not for the first time I wondered whether I would be able to wrap both hands around them.

"I'll get back to you later, Monique," I said as I hung up on her.

"Come in, Jorge." I motioned him in. "Do I have time to get changed?"

"Yeah, we got about fifteen minutes before we need to leave for the airport."

"Make yourself comfortable, I'll be ready in five."

Jorge chuckled. "Sure you will."

Closing my door, I changed out of my funeral clothes and into my assistant clothes, comfortable and nondescript. As an assistant to some of the most attention needy people in the world I had learned long ago to dress as if I was fading into the background. If I was noticed then I had made a mistake. Pulling my hair back into the classic ponytail and slipping on comfortable shoes, I grabbed my bag and headed out.

"See, I told you, five minutes. You should have more faith in me."

The smile on my face froze when I found Griffin in my apartment, glaring at Jorge, who was quite comfortably lounging on my couch with a drink, looking like he spent quite a bit of time there.

"Oh hi, Griffin, what are you doing here?"

With his hands on hips he turned his glare from Jorge to me. "Tomas Burnelli told me about your little incident at the wake, so I was checking to make sure you were okay."

"Tomas worries too much, nothing happened to us. We just hid in a closet while Catarina's assistant was talking to the guy who looked like he kicked puppies for fun."

"I was just on my way to see Peter but I wanted to check on you first," Griffin said.

"Oh sure." I shrugged. "Not the first time I've had to avoid someone by hiding in a closet."

Griffin looked from me to Jorge's grinning face. "So exactly what is happening here?" he asked.

"Jorge and I have a job to do for the rest of the day and tonight. He was sent to pick me up and I just needed to get changed from the funeral.

"Yeah, that's not going to happen. You won't be doing the job," Griffin said.

Jorge choked on the glass of water he had been drinking.

"Dude," he muttered, "so uncool."

"Jorge, could you please give me a moment?" I asked sweetly, although the look I was shooting in Griffin's direction was anything but sweet.

"Sure, sure," said Jorge, "I'll just wait for you in the limo." As he walked past Griffin I heard him mutter under his breath. "Dead man walking."

He closed the door gently behind him but not before shooting me a pointed look.

"So was there a real reason for this visit or did you just intend to humiliate me in front of my co-worker?" I asked.

Griffin held up his hands in a placating gesture. "I didn't say that right, I'm sorry."

"Oh, you're sorry for telling me I couldn't do my job." I wanted to be clear on this so that I knew exactly the reason I was furious with him or whether I should just go nuclear.

Griffin looked at me sheepishly. "Well no, you can't go and especially not with him."

Nuclear it was then.

"How dare you tell me what I can do with my job. You do not have any right to do that. You especially don't have any right to tell me who I can and can't work with.

Anyway, what is your problem with Jorge? He is one of the nicest guys that I know. I'm actually happy when I get to work with him because then I can concentrate on my job and I know he'll help me if I need it."

"He's not who you think he is, I can't say anything more than that but I don't want you anywhere near that guy," Griffin said with that infuriatingly calm voice he seemed to employ with me regularly.

"No," I said.

"Excuse me." Griffin looked startled. I shrugged, the anger still there but I wasn't going to argue about this. A part of me marveled that he honestly seemed to expect me to just fall into line with his edicts.

"No, you don't get to tell me what to do and expect me to do it. I will take any suggestions you give under advisement but you do not get to give me orders and expect me to obey you."

Griffin pulled his hand through his hair, his frustration evident. "I'm not trying to control you. I'm trying to keep you safe which seems to be a full time job. In less than a couple of hours you almost walk in on what sounds to have been a shake down by a very, and I can't emphasize this enough, very, bad man. Now you're about to get into a car and spend the day and night with a man that I do not want you anywhere near. I don't want you hurt, not in any way. I know you're angry with me but you can't ask me to stand by when I see you may be walking into a dangerous situation."

He had stepped closer and looking into his eyes I could see that he was dealing with emotions that he wasn't overly familiar with.

"This is one of those moments," I said quietly.

"What moments?" Griffin asked, probably a bit more harshly than he meant to.

I reached up and kissed him on the cheek. "This is one of those moments where you tell me your opinion and you trust me to make the right decision. I don't know what you think you know about Jorge but I can guarantee that he is not that person."

"Are you willing to bet your life and your safety on that?" Griffin said harshly.

"Yes," I said quietly. "I exasperate you, don't I?" I asked as I wound my arms around him."

He put his arms around my shoulders and held me tight. "You terrify me," he mumbled as he kissed the top of my head. I put my hand in his and pulled him towards the door.

"Now you need to let me do my job, I have to go."

"I'm not going to win this one, am I?" said Griffin.

I looked at him seriously. "You were never going to win."

"Does this qualify as our first fight? Griffin grinned ruefully.

I smiled back. "You must have the memory of a goldfish, we've done nothing but argue since the first day we met. Now you are going to walk me down to the car and you are not going to pull Jorge aside for a quiet word."

Griffin quirked an eyebrow and I laughed.

"Don't look at me like that. I know you were thinking it. You can't get anything past me, Detective."

Chapter Twelve

At the limo, Jorge opened the door for me and winked, purely for Griffin's benefit. I had to stop myself from rolling my eyes. I seemed to be surrounded by men who loved the idea of annoying each other. Griffin glared at Jorge and then stopped me and gave me a hard and fast kiss.

"Be safe," he murmured.

"I will," I said and before he could think of another way to try and stop me, I got into the limo.

Jorge settled in across from me. Once the car started up, Jorge cleared his throat.

"So you've still got your cop boyfriend."

"Looks like it," I said.

There was silence again. Jorge looked nervous as he peered out of the tinted windows.

"Did he tell you why he didn't want you to do this job?" Jorge asked.

Jorge had only ever been good to me and I wanted to be honest with him.

"He didn't want me working with you," I said bluntly.

"Did he tell you why?" asked Jorge.

I shook my head.

"He knows something about you but he wouldn't tell me what it was. Suffice to say he believes that you are a possible danger to me. He has a tendency to overreact when it comes to my safety."

Jorge chuckled. "That's a bit of an understatement. You came on this job anyway. Doesn't it worry you that he might know something about me that you don't?"

I focused on Jorge. "No, it doesn't worry me. I've worked with you before and I have never felt anything but safe around you. I don't know what may have happened in your past to make Griffin worry about you, but the man I work with now, I feel completely safe with him. If I have to babysit a rich, entitled drug addled socialite for the next eighteen hours of my life there is no one else that I would prefer to do it with."

Jorge leaned back and crossed his arms. "I did some pretty bad things when I was younger," he said.

"You don't have to tell me anything," I said softly.

"I want to. Monique knows all this and she gave me a chance, now I'm going to take a chance on you. I did a lot of stupid things when I was younger. Got involved with very bad people, ran with gangs, did a lot of horrible things. I was always pretty huge so I became a thug and a bully and I was good at it. I scare people now when I'm not trying to. Can you imagine what I did when I didn't care about hurting them? Never got convicted of anything, no one was ever willing to testify against me, that's how bad a person I was."

Jorge closed his eyes and breathed in as if he was fighting himself.

"What changed?" I asked softly.

"A few years back I went into some corner store, was throwing my weight around, threatening the owner, not wanting anything, just being bored. This woman fronts me, tells me to get out. To me she was this tiny thing and I was overconfident. I went to push her out the way and to this day I don't know what she did but I ended up on my back looking up at the ceiling."

"How did she do it?" I asked.

"US Marine Corps. Can you imagine it? The last thing I was expecting but there she is standing over me and she says to me 'this isn't you Jorge, you're better than this.' For the first time in my life in a very long time I felt ashamed of what I did."

"Who was she?" I asked.

"Her name was Linda. I went to school with her when I was a kid. It seems that I once protected her from some kid who was bullying her. I didn't remember but she did. She remembered me as someone who protected those weaker than himself. She thought of me as someone to look up to and admire. She joined the Corps and was home on leave to see her family. After she dumped me on my backside she dragged me out of there. Seems she was the only person in my life who had ever seen me as a hero. By the time that night was over I wanted her to see me as that hero again. She saved my life and my soul that night. I married her six months later."

"Where is she now?" I asked.

"She's deployed at the moment."

"Must be tough," I said.

"Which part?" Jorge said humorlessly. "Being a military spouse or knowing that the woman I love more than breathing is currently in a very dangerous part of the world."

"Did you think about joining up?" I asked.

"Not for a second," said Jorge. "If we'd both been deployed we would never see each other. This way she comes home and I'm right here waiting for her."

I felt tears well up in my eyes. "That is the most beautiful story," I said, reaching for a tissue. "She must be really lovely."

Jorge laughed. "Don't get me wrong, she has a temper that goes off like a rocket and a mouth on her that makes me wince sometimes, but I work hard every day to be a man she can be proud of. That is why, despite what the cop believes, I am not that man any more and I never will be again. There is no way in hell that I am willing to disappoint that woman. I'm not that brave."

"Thank you for telling me," I said.

"You remind me a bit of my Linda," Jorge said. "You're loyal to a fault and when you believe in someone you don't let anyone tell you different."

"You're sweet," I said.

Jorge laughed. "And you are one of the few people

who actually thinks that about me," he said. "So, why are you still with the cop?" He suddenly changed the topic. "Last time we talked about him you didn't think there was a chance for you."

I hesitated, wondering how to deal with that question. To be perfectly honest, the last time Jorge and I had discussed my relationship with Griffin, I hadn't really been in a relationship with him. He had actually been working undercover as my fake boyfriend. At the time I had been blackmailed into helping him. So, out of spite over the fact that I was having to lie to people I counted as my friends, I may have intimated that I would be breaking up with him in the near future due to his inadequacies in certain areas. I winced at the memory.

"We're kind of working it out at the moment," I said, hoping that he didn't probe any further. Of course, I should have remembered that this was Jorge.

"Last time we spoke I believe that your exact words were that he didn't quite live up to advertising." Jorge grinned.

"Things are different now," I said quietly. "I'm not really sure where things are going. We've both got a lot to work out."

"The question is do you think he's worth it?"

I thought about it and nodded slowly. "You know, I really do think he might be."

"Then that's all that's important," he said, looking out the window. "Just remember that you deserve awesome, don't ever settle for anything less."

I grinned. "You know you don't look it but you are really good at girl talk."

Jorge gave me a disgusted look. "Now you're just being mean."

Chapter Thirteen

Waiting in the airport for Blythe Stanton, I was thankful to have Jorge standing next to me. It meant I was spared the normal crush of people. Between his size, his tattoos and his 'don't mess with me' expression, people tended to give him a wide berth, and I was standing close enough to be caught up in that circle of intimidation.

Finally, once all the other passengers had disembarked, I spotted Blythe Stanton leaning heavily on a flight attendant as they walked down the hallway. Blythe appeared unsteady as she stumbled along on impossibly high stilettos. Jorge and I went forward and while Jorge grabbed the bag that the flight attendant had been holding, I took the attendant's position at Blythe's side and put her arm around my shoulders.

"Who are you?" she slurred.

"My name is Trudie and this is Jorge. Your father asked us to meet you and help you while you are in LA." I smiled reassuringly.

"Okay," she slurred dumbly and slumped against me.

"I think she may have overindulged on the plane," the flight attendant said apologetically, before taking her first opportunity to leave.

I looked at Jorge and he smiled. I knew what he was thinking. If she fell asleep until her flight home, this could be the easiest money we had ever made. Jorge took a position in front of us and we tried to discreetly make our way through the airport. Avoiding the paparazzi proved to be impossible but Jorge's sheer bulk and the way Blythe's face slumped forward with her long blonde hair covering it, we were able to mitigate the potential damage. Of course, as usual, my face was front and center. For someone who wasn't famous, I seemed to spend a lot of time being photographed.

Once settled in the limo, I turned to Jorge. "Where to now?"

"Monique organized a suite in a hotel for us to use as a base camp until we get her on the plane tomorrow morning."

"What do you think our chances are of getting her on the plane?" I asked.

Jorge cracked his knuckles and had a smile on his face that, if I didn't know him better, I would think was slightly terrifying.

"She'll be on the plane," he said.

Good to know. Monique as usual had organized a suite which was perfect. The decor was slightly dated but its most important asset was that it was private and not one that always had a score of paparazzi hanging around. Despite the fact that she had never succeeded as either an actress or a singer, in fact the less said about her singing career the better, Blythe Stanton was a socialite heiress who had become famous for having a lifestyle that people envied. Before her life had taken its spectacular slide downhill, she had seemed to have it all. Now, as I looked at her passed out, face down on the bed, I wondered what had happened to cause this. Closing the bedroom door I found Jorge going through her luggage on the couch.

"Find anything yet?" I asked.

"No drugs yet if that's what you mean," said Jorge.

"Anything else I should be panicking about?" I asked as I crossed over to the mini bar.

"No, standard gear for an out of control socialite. Lots of makeup products. Seriously, how can one woman use all this stuff?"

I smiled at him. "Don't look at me, I'm more of a natural kind of girl. If I can't get ready in ten minutes then it's too much trouble."

Jorge pulled up a tiny scrap of cloth. "Where is she going to wear this?"

I touched the fabric. I may not be able to afford this kind of garment but I'd been around enough people who could to know that it was very expensive and very exclusive.

"I am guessing that is what she will be wearing tonight."

"She's going to freeze to death," Jorge muttered.

"Yes, but this club belongs to husband number three doesn't it?"

Jorge nodded.

"Doesn't matter what she has to go through. That first moment he sees her, she wants him to know exactly what he missed out on."

"It's a woman thing isn't it?" Jorge asked.

"Absolutely," I said. "I'm pretty low maintenance but any time I see my ex, I make sure I look as good as is humanly possible. It's a pride thing."

Jorge stuffed the shimmery piece of fabric back in the luggage.

"Well, the luggage looks clean so, fortunately for us, she's obviously smart enough not to try to smuggle drugs over the border."

"Doesn't mean she hasn't already organized for someone to supply her here."

Jorge sat down and watched as I gathered up all the alcohol in the mini bar. "What are you doing?"

"Making this room a dry one," I said as there was a knock on the door. Jorge opened the door to find room service with a tray.

"Uh, Trudie?" he questioned.

"That's perfect," I said as the tray cart rolled in.

"And if you could remove these." I handed the small bottles over to the waiter. "And please don't replace them for the duration of the stay."

When he left I lifted the covers on the plates.

"I don't know about you but I've had hardly anything to eat all day, so I thought I'd grab us both something before we had to tackle tonight."

Jorge grinned and grabbed his plate. "I could get used to doing these jobs with you," he said.

"Experience," I said as I started in on my gourmet burger, definitely a step up from my usual hamburger. "I need to eat or I start getting very cranky and I can't do my job if I'm cranky."

As we were inhaling the food I heard a noise coming from the bedroom.

"Looks like you're up," said Jorge.

Shoving the last of the burger in my mouth, I made my way to the door and knocked gently on it.

"Miss Stanton, are you okay?" When I was greeted with silence I knocked again. "Miss Stanton, my name is Trudie Eyre. I'm your assistant while you're in LA." Still silence. "Miss Stanton, I'm coming in now. I need to see that you are okay."

I opened the door slowly, preparing myself to duck if any projectiles came my way. Sometimes walking into the bedroom of someone who was coming down from a chemically induced high could be dangerous. Luckily, most projectiles that had come my way while walking into a bedroom consisted of pillows and cushions, although there was that time when I had a pair of handcuffs hurled in my direction. On the plus side they hadn't been police issue, no, these had been the fluffy ones that could be bought online. That being said, they had made quite a menacing thud on the door when I'd pulled it shut, proving my reaction time was pretty good. As I cautiously entered the room I could see the shape under the covers and hear a disembodied groaning.

"Miss Stanton," I said cautiously. "Is there anything I can do to help?"

The covers were ripped back and a bleary eyed socialite peered at me dolefully from the bed. "Who the bloody hell are you and where am I?"

Great, I love the blackout ones.

"Do you remember getting on a plane, Miss Stanton?"

Her forehead wrinkled as she tried to remember. Usually I work with women who are incapable of that expression due to Botox injections. It threw me off my game for a second.

"I think I do," she said and I could see that she was concentrating really hard.

"You're in LA. Do you know why?"

Another frown. "I was at rehab and my friend Jane called. She told me that Carl was opening a club in LA."

"Carl is your ex-husband?" I prompted and was surprised to see tears in her eyes.

"We were going to do it together and I screwed it up. Now he's doing it on his own. I've lost him and it's all my fault."

She started wailing and the door got flung open and Jorge filled the doorway. He took one look at me standing there helplessly and the woman crying her eyes out on the bed, and he turned around and closed the door. Sitting next to her on the bed I awkwardly put my arm around her shoulder and patted her.

"There, there, we'll work it out."

"You don't understand," she gasped out between heaving sobs. "I wanted him back. I went to rehab to show him I could get better, but when I heard he was opening the club without me it was like he moved on. He didn't need me any more. I left rehab and headed for the airport. I was waiting for my plane and I headed for the bar. I don't remember much after that."

"Blythe, I need you to tell me if you took anything other than the alcohol."

"No, I don't think so, but I started drinking again. I've lost him forever."

And the wailing started again. I could feel the sound of it reverberating through my skull.

"No," I said loudly. The wailing kept going.

"For the love of… Will you shut up," I yelled.

The wailing stopped mid cry and two round eyes looked up at me.

"Feeling sorry for yourself is not going to get him back. If you really want him and this isn't just some stupid pride thing, I will help you, but you have to make your decision now."

Blythe gulped and nodded her head slowly. "He's my soul mate, I can't go on without him."

I stopped myself from grimacing. I'm not a big fan of the whole soul mate idea. I generally find that people who have found their soul mates have a tendency to let the universe decide their romantic moves. Never a good plan in my opinion. Of course, the guy I thought was my soul mate had ended up being a jerk, so it could just be that I'm a bit cynical. I pulled back the covers.

"Very well, if we are going to do this, the first thing is to sober you up a bit. Into the shower, try to get rid of the alcohol smell and when you come out, I'll have some food and coffee waiting for you.

She nodded quietly and pulled herself out of bed. I watched her walk to the bathroom noting that she wasn't too unsteady on her feet. Closing the door quietly, I found Jorge looking pensive.

"Is she okay?" he asked.

"No, not really," I said as I went over to start the coffee machine working.

Jorge tried again. "She looked really upset. Does that mean we're not going anywhere tonight? We just need to get her on that flight."

"I like your optimism, but plans have changed."

Jorge looked at me suspiciously. "What do you mean, plans have changed?"

"We have a goal for the night. We're going to go to that club opening and we are going to help Blythe Stanton get her husband back."

The look on Jorge's face was comical and I had to stop myself from laughing as I worked on wrestling the complicated coffee machine into submission.

"Uh, Trudie, I don't really think that kind of thing is in our job description."

"Oh, Jorge," I said. "Sweet, innocent, deluded, Jorge. Our job description consists of making our client's life as smooth and easy as possible. Our options include helping that woman get her husband back or listen to her wailing for the next," I checked my watch, "eleven hours. Is that really how you want to spend that time?"

Jorge grimaced. "I guess not," he said, although to my way of thinking it sounded more like a question than a statement.

By the time Blythe eventually got out of the shower I was beginning to rethink my plan. After sitting her down with coffee and water I sat across from her.

"Is this really what you want to do now?" I asked.

"What do you mean?" she replied mutinously.

"Well," I said, slowly trying to decide how to word this. Jorge was deliberately avoiding any part of this conversation, and refused to even look me in the eye. "Do you think you're in the best condition to try to get your ex-husband back?" I hated to say it but I had to be brutally honest. The woman was going through rehab and had just fallen off the wagon in a spectacular way, and she looked it.

"You don't think he'll want me?" she whispered quietly and I could see the tears welling in her eyes.

"No, no," I said quickly, hoping I could head off the wailing that looked like it was about to start again. "I'm just saying that maybe we need a little help tonight with makeup and dressing."

"I've got a dress," she said, jumping up and pulling out the tiny scrap of silver fabric.

I looked at Jorge and he just shrugged.

"That's a lovely dress," I said. "And it would look great on you."

It would, she had the perfect figure for that dress. If we

were just going out for a night on the prowl it would be the perfect dress. We weren't going for a night on the prowl though. We had a mission and that required something more targeted than the wide net approach that a dress like that signified.

"Is there any outfit that Carl particularly liked?" I asked.

"I have the dress with me that I was wearing the day he said he loved me," she said quietly. "I haven't been able to wear it since the divorce, but I carry it everywhere with me. I can't seem to let it go."

Well, that pretty much broke my heart and I could see that it affected Jorge too. To carry around a dress you had no intention of wearing simply because it reminded you of a wonderful memory. That kind of story was guaranteed to tug at the heartstrings. Blythe went into her room and I looked over at Jorge.

"Fine," he said gruffly. "We're going to get her old man back but we are never speaking of this again."

"Agreed," I nodded.

Blythe came out with a surprisingly simple dress that skimmed her knees and only gave a hint of her cleavage. It was a dress that whispered of the promise of seduction rather than shouting it. I could see why Carl had been taken with it.

"I think that would be perfect," I said.

Chapter Fourteen

That left us with the makeup situation. Blythe Stanton was an attractive woman. Unfortunately, she was not looking her best at the moment. Circles rimmed her eyes and her skin had broken out and was dry in areas. I know that love is not supposed to be all about the physical, but a nice package helps, especially for a mission like this. There's a reason why plastic surgery is such a lucrative industry in this town.

I pulled out my cell and called the one person I thought could help. An hour later there was a knock at the door.

Throwing it wide open, I welcomed Tomas and Helena into the room.

"Hello, Helena," I said, after giving Tomas a hug.

"You're Trudie," she said. "I remember you. You are Eric's friend.

I nodded as I got swamped by the uniqueness that was Helena. It may have been overstating things to say I had been Eric's friend. Eric had been the husband of one of my clients, and for two weeks before he met his untimely end he had made my life very difficult. Helena, of course, had only met Eric after his death when she had been hired as a funeral cosmetologist to fix the damage only a bullet hole to the head could do. Despite her unusual ways, Helena was a genius when it came to make up and what she could hide.

"Eric has such a beautiful spirit. Is this who I'm helping today?" she asked, her eyes wide when she saw Blythe.

"Yes, Helena. Blythe needs to look beautiful tonight, we're trying to reunite her with her husband," I said.

Helena clapped her hands together. "Of course, I will make her as beautiful as Eric," she said as she took Blythe into the bedroom and started chatting away about all the people she had worked with.

"Is she going to say anything to Blythe about all those people being dead when she worked on them?" I muttered to Tomas.

"Helena doesn't really distinguish between dead and alive," said Tomas quietly. "As far as she is concerned they all have beautiful spirits and they all talk to her."

"Great," I muttered.

"You wouldn't have called me if you didn't know how good she was," Tomas reminded me.

"I know," I said.

Jorge, who was standing at the door to the bedroom watching Helena and Blythe, turned around.

"She just told Blythe to stop breathing as it was distracting her. Is that normal?

I shook my head. "For Helena, that's pretty normal. I'd better be in there and make sure that she doesn't decide to stop that pesky breathing from happening."

"She won't do that," scoffed Tomas, then he stopped and looked like he was contemplating what I'd just said. "No, of course she wouldn't."

Within no time Helena clapped her hands and turned Blythe around.

"Perfect," I said and Helena's eyes sparkled. It was perfect. Helena had erased the short term damage that Blythe had caused and managed to make her look completely natural.

"She is a genius," I said as I watched Helena start dancing around the room, catching Blythe's hand and pulling her along. Watching Helena was always like watching a free spirit who didn't let the normal problems of life touch her. Seeing Blythe smile as she was being led around the room, I couldn't help but think that we all could use a bit of what Helena had.

Sitting in the limo outside the club, I could see Blythe was no longer feeling the effects of Helena's carefree attitude to life as she was chewing on her bottom lip.

"Last chance to turn around," I said. "You don't have to do this. You can go back to rehab, finish the program and face him when you are in a better place."

"I want to do this," she said quietly as she squared her shoulders.

As the door opened, Jorge went out first to provide protection. Blythe followed him and I went after her. Getting into the club was no problem, even without an invitation. It rarely is for my clients. Being whisked to the VIP area, Jorge and I kept a close eye on Blythe. The darkness of the club and the lights bouncing on the dancers had a hypnotic effect and could be distracting. In the middle of the VIP area we found our target. Unfortunately, he was surrounded by beautiful women who seemed to be very friendly with him. Blythe stumbled slightly and I put out my arm to steady her. Pain creased her features.

"I didn't even think that he'd move on," she whispered as Jorge stood in front of us, blocking anyone from seeing. "I am such an idiot. Of course he's moved on. Why would he wait for me to sort myself out? Let's just get out of here."

"Are you sure that's what you want?" I whispered back. "You're here now, don't you want to at least give it a try?"

"I think I've humiliated myself enough in my life," Blythe said tightly. "I'm not going to exacerbate the disaster that is my existence by getting into a fight in a club over my ex-husband."

"Good to see your spirit," I said, "but I wasn't talking about fighting for him. You could just go up to him and say hello."

Blythe shook her head. "No," she said. "I think that I just need to go home. I've screwed things up for myself enough. I should never have got on that plane. I just got it into my head that if I could just get him back then everything would be okay. I need to stand up on my own for a change. I want him back so badly, but I won't humiliate myself to do it," she said with the beginning of tears in her eyes.

I nodded sharply and tapped Jorge on the shoulder. "We're out of here," I said. Showing himself to be the consummate professional, Jorge did not sigh or roll his eyes at the sudden change in plans.

As we started to walk away I noticed that Carl looked up and saw Blythe. In that second I saw adoration flash across his face when he looked at the woman I was following. My breath caught and I pulled Blythe to a stop.

"What?" she said, and I indicated to Carl with my head.

The second he caught her eye he was on his feet, shrugging off the women who had been vying for his attention.

"Blythe," he said as he got to us and pulled her into a hug. "It is so good to see you. What are you doing here?"

Blythe smiled sweetly and I could see Carl almost being taken out at the knees.

"I wanted to see your club, Carl," she said, "Congratulations, I'm so happy for you."

"I've missed you so much," he said roughly. "I can't believe you're here, I thought you were done with us."

Blythe hesitated. "I'm so sorry, Carl," she said, her eyes once again filling with tears. "I messed everything up. I should never have given up on us."

"But you're back," Carl said.

"Only for a few hours," said Blythe. "Then I'm going back to rehab and I'm going to fix my life."

She sounded resolute and for the first time since I met her coming off the plane, I started to think that maybe there was a chance that Blythe could actually succeed. I had seen many of my clients going in and coming out of rehab and I had learned that only a few actually make it. Those that did needed to find something inside themselves which made them want to get clean. As I watched Blythe and Carl, I could see that Blythe had found what she needed.

Carl cleared his throat. "Can we talk?" he said. "Not here, in my office upstairs."

Blythe smiled. "Not tonight, Carl," she said. "You have your opening, we can talk when I get back if you still want to."

Carl grabbed Blythe's hand and started leading her away. "No, you are more important to me than this opening. We are going to sort this out now," he said as he started dragging her along. He didn't get far before he ran into the massive wall that was Jorge.

"Is this what you want, Blythe?" I asked, watching as security started making a beeline for us.

Blythe nodded, her smile blinding. "Yes," she said, "I really do want this. Stay here and I'll be out soon."

I nodded at Jorge and he stepped aside. Carl led a giggling Blythe up the stairs to his office.

"I hope we've done the right thing," grumbled Jorge as he sat down at a small table which overlooked the dance floor.

I sat down next to him. "What else were we going to do?" I asked him. "She's a grown woman and she's making her own decisions."

"Yeah, but what if she has sex with him when we're supposed to be taking care of her?" Jorge said.

"Our job description does not include being a chastity belt," I said dryly. "Our job involves getting her on that plane and back to rehab. That is what we intend to do. Until then we wait and amuse ourselves without having too much fun."

"Great," said Jorge. "I'll go get us some drinks that we won't enjoy very much."

"Thanks," I said.

Watching the dancing below, I was surprised when someone sat next to me at the table.

"You were at Catarina's funeral today weren't you?" asked a slurred voice.

I looked at my new companion and she looked familiar.

"I'm sorry," I said. "Were you there this morning?"

She smiled and held out her hand, a little shakily. "I'm Antonia. I went to school with Catarina."

I gripped her hand "Trudie, I was there to support a friend who knew Catarina."

"The gorgeous English guy," she said, smiling. "Yes, he looked like he would be Catarina's type."

I shrugged because really what could I say, Edwin had been exactly Catarina's type.

Antonia smiled as she took another drink. She looked pleasantly hammered.

"It was a boring funeral," she said slowly. "I was sure there were going to be a lot more people there, just to make sure she was really dead."

"I didn't know Catarina at all," I said with what I hoped was disinterest. "Wasn't she well liked?"

Antonia drew herself up as if in shock. "She was hated by everyone she met. She used people and she stole from them. I knew her since high school and I don't think she ever did a selfless thing or had an original thought in her entire life."

"That can't be true," I said. "She wrote those movies and she won all those awards. I remember everyone saying that she was some kind of prodigy."

Antonia snorted. "I knew Catarina. There is no way that she wrote those movies. Her only talent was being a con artist and a thief. In high school she stole boyfriends and clothes. She cheated in every class she was in. Her greatest gift was being able to convince everyone that she was so talented and hard working. I'm amazed it took this long before somebody killed her."

"Any idea who that could have been?" I asked, spotting Jorge coming towards me and indicating that he keep back.

"Catarina was a horrible human being. I was her best friend in high school and she stole my boyfriend for no reason other than he was there and I wasn't. And she liked me. She had no limits as to what she would do. You know how people have that thing in their head that tells them what's right from wrong."

I nodded.

"Catarina didn't have that. Everyone on this planet was here to do what she wanted."

"Hey, babe." Some bearded hipster wannabe threw an arm around Antonia's shoulders. "Why did you wander off? I got worried about you."

Antonia giggled inanely.

"This is my boyfriend, David," she said, "and this is..."

"Trudie," I supplied.

"Yes, Trudie. She was at the funeral this morning."

David rolled his eyes. "Wasn't that the biggest waste of time?" he grumbled. "I thought there would have been far more directors or producers there. I'm getting more networking opportunities here and it's a much better party."

You know you're in a good place when a funeral is considered a networking event.

"Come on, Toni," David said. "Let's dance."

Still juggling her drink, Antonia kept giggling and followed David to the dance floor. Jorge slipped into the seat she had just vacated and passed over a water to me.

"What was that all about?" he asked, opening his own bottle of water.

"Some woman, she recognized me from Catarina Badal's funeral this morning," I said.

"Another funeral," Jorge said thoughtfully.

I peered over the top of my bottle at him. "You want to say something, don't you?"

"Nah," he said. "Well, it's just that people around the agency are kind of starting to talk about the body count you seem to be racking up."

I placed the bottle gently on the table. "Body count?" I queried.

Jorge started to look uncomfortable. "I'm not saying it

bothers me, I'm just saying that you're beginning to get a bit of a reputation. Fact is, despite the fact the guy seems like a douche, I'm kind of glad you're seeing that cop. At least he can keep an eye on you, you know, make sure that you don't get hurt."

"You know, people die all the time," I said, starting to feel defensive. "I didn't actually kill anyone."

"Of course not," said Jorge soothingly, obviously regretting his part in instigating this line of conversation.

"What exactly are people saying?" I asked.

Jorge hesitated, obviously trying to decide what he should and shouldn't say.

"Tell me the truth," I said quietly.

Jorge sighed. "I've heard you being called the Grim Reaper. The rumor is that people who annoy you die suddenly."

"If that were really true," I said, "believe me, the body count would be much higher. If anyone calls me the Grim Reaper again you can quote me on that."

"I already said that," said Jorge. "Considering the fact you seem to be signed up for the worst cases that the agency gets, I figured if you had some weird voodoo power killing people, there would be a lot more unexplained deaths."

"They're not unexplained," I said dourly. "The police arrested people in all of the cases."

"Catarina Badal?" Jorge queried.

"Okay, the police haven't caught anyone for that one yet, but they will. I didn't even know the woman so there is no way I can be blamed for that."

Jorge grunted with a smile and took another drink.

"I thought Monique put you with me tonight because you're the nice one," I complained.

Jorge shrugged. "Truthfully, your reputation makes some of the other security guys a little nervous about working with you. Lucky for you, I don't believe it and I'm just that brave."

I looked at him sourly. "Considering my reputation, I'm not sure giving me attitude is a smart idea."

"I'm a man who lives on the edge," he said, grinning at me.

Chapter Fifteen

When my head finally hit the pillow at seven the next morning, I groaned with how good it felt. Jorge and I had accomplished our mission of getting Blythe Stanton on the plane back to rehab. Carl had accompanied us to the airport as well. After spending the entire night in his office, they had decided to give their marriage another go. That started with Blythe getting herself clean, so she bravely got back on to the plane. We then had to deal with Carl, who was so overwhelmingly grateful for the part we had played in helping him get Blythe back, that he got weepy with us in the limo when we were taking him home. Poor Jorge had looked uncomfortable as the man had hugged him repeatedly on the way back. For me that sight alone had made the whole night worth it. The only thing that would have made it better is if I'd managed to immortalize the moment with a photo. Although, considering the dirty look Jorge was shooting in my direction as I was obviously trying very hard not to laugh, I don't think my camera would have survived the experience.

Just as I was drifting off, my cell rang. Drowsily, I slapped my hand on the bedside table and knocked the phone on the floor. Faced with the choice as to whether I would get up and answer the phone or cover my head with the pillow and go back to sleep, I decided that no one was more important to me than sleep at the moment. Finally, the ringing stopped and I snuggled down further into the covers and drifted off, only to be woken suddenly when the covers were ripped off my bed.

"What the...?" I gasped as I looked up into Crystal's smiling face.

"Get dressed, we're going to Vegas," she said as I tried

to pull the covers back over me.

"I'm not going anywhere," I groaned. "I just got home from work and I need to sleep.

Crystal turned and grabbed my overnight bag and started throwing clothes in. "You have to come. I'm getting married and I need you with me."

I laughed. "I must be more tired than I thought. I'm beginning to hallucinate. For a moment there I thought you said that you were going to get married." I dropped my head back to the pillow. "Go away and leave my key here."

"Not going to happen," said Crystal, still packing my clothes. "Edwin and I are getting married today and you're going to be the bridesmaid and best man. You are going to be standing there so I don't panic and run at the last minute."

Something in Crystal's voice finally made it through my sleep deprived brain and I sat back up. "You're getting married?" I said.

"Yes."

"To Edwin."

"Yes."

"In Vegas."

"Yes."

"Have you told your dad?"

Crystal gulped. "No."

"Do you think you should?"

"No," and in case I didn't get it, she shook her head emphatically.

"Why the rush to get married?" I asked. "Don't you want a big wedding, have your family there, except your mom of course."

Crystal grabbed hold of my hand and forced me to look at her. "I don't want the big wedding, I don't want to wait. I know, in my soul, that Edwin is the one for me. I've known it forever but I just didn't want to risk doing anything to our friendship. If I wait and get caught up in the whole wedding fiasco, I may run or do something really stupid. I may find out that I'm a little too much like my mom. I just want him. Do you understand?"

I nodded, tears forming in my eyes. It was crazy but it was so sweet. "Crystal, you know I'm your friend and I'm with you all the way and it is only as your friend that I am saying this, but have you really thought this through?"

"Yes," she said.

"Fine, I'm with you. Just get me some coffee."

By the time we got to the airport I was on my second cup of coffee and was feeling much better. In no time at all we were in Vegas. Racing straight from the airport to a Vegas chapel, it hit me that Crystal and Edwin were actually going to do this. Admittedly there seemed to be some undue haste around the whole thing but they were actually going to do this. As we stood in front of the duly authorized celebrant of the state of Nevada, a part of me envied how sure the two of them were that they were making the right decision. Despite Crystal's fears that she would be tempted to run at the last minute, she stood next to Edwin and recited her vows in a strong voice. Edwin rushed through his vows as if desperate to finally make Crystal his. I provided the happy tears as my two friends promised to love each other forever. When Edwin swept Crystal into his arms and kissed her at the end of the ceremony, I felt a tiny bit of jealousy. Edwin looked at Crystal like he couldn't believe his luck. I hugged them both.

"I am so happy for you," I said fiercely.

When Crystal was a child, whenever her mother wanted to squeeze a bit of money out of her father, she would exercise her maternal rights and Crystal would be spirited away to Vegas. How long her stay was depended largely on how big a payoff her mother was looking for. Of course once she had her daughter in Vegas, Crystal had been pretty much left to her own devices. As a result Crystal had a good knowledge of parts of Vegas which didn't necessarily show up on the tourist map. This included a little Italian restaurant where the three of us toasted a great day and some truly exceptional food. As the morning wore on I could feel my eyelids growing heavier until Crystal clicked her fingers in front of me.

"We need to get you to bed," she said.

"On your wedding night," I said, smiling. "I know we're friends but that's going a bit too far."

Edwin grinned.

"Very funny," said Crystal. "We'll take you to the hotel and you can get some sleep."

"No," I said. "You guys are having fun. It's your day. I can take a cab to the hotel, no problems, and you can enjoy the rest of your day."

The two of them protested but I finally managed to find a cab and make it back to the hotel.

Crystal had organized a suite for the three of us but at the front desk I ordered my own room. The three of us were close but I knew the friendship etiquette for sharing a suite on your wedding night was kind of gray. So they didn't worry, I sent a text message to Crystal as I unlocked the door. Dropping my bag, I felt like I was not going to make it to the bed. I am not the sort of person who deals with lack of sleep well. If I don't get a decent night's sleep, I am a bitter and angry person until I can put my head down on a pillow.

Just as I started towards the bed there was a knock on the door. I contemplated ignoring it but the knock happened again, this time more insistent. I grabbed the door handle ready to politely tell whoever was knocking to go to hell. I was stunned to see the mobster debt collector from the funeral standing at the doorway. In a moment he had grabbed my arm, spun me around and was holding me against his chest.

"This isn't gonna hurt a bit," he murmured in my ear.

I struggled desperately as I felt a small prick in the side of my neck. I started to scream and a hand was clasped over my mouth. As I fought against the iron bars holding me, I could see the room getting darker, like storm clouds crossing the sky until everything went black.

Chapter Sixteen

Opening my eyes was a struggle. I felt like I should use my arms but my whole body felt heavy. When I finally got my eyes open, I found that I was lying on a hard wood floor. My stomach started rolling and I felt like I was going to be sick.

"Oh good, you're awake," I heard from above me.

I had to concentrate to move my head in the direction of the voice. The voice came from behind a desk and I couldn't see who was talking. I was going to have to sit up. Concentrating hard, I managed to pull my arms up underneath me. I levered on my hands and felt my stomach starting to rebel again. Pushing up into a sitting position, I squinted my eyes and saw a well-dressed man walking towards me. His suit said businessman but there was no way that was all he was. Every move he made seemed to scream danger and I wasn't just saying that because I'd been kidnapped and ended up on his floor.

"Here, I think you're going to need this," he said, passing me a glass of water.

I looked at it suspiciously.

"If I had any nefarious plans for you I could have carried them out while you were passed out on my floor," he said. "I did not mean for you to be here. One of my colleague's made an error in judgment. I am now trying to rectify it."

"And yet I don't see any police or paramedics," I croaked.

He smiled crookedly. "Unfortunately, my colleague's rash actions have put me in a bit of a difficult position. I have a certain reputation which could count against me if I contacted the police. However, I was starting to get concerned. I was assured the drug cocktail you were injected with would only last a few hours and you've been out considerably longer than that."

"How long?" I asked.

"You've been unconscious for approximately nine hours. If it makes you feel better you have been checked by a doctor."

"I've been laying on a floor for nine hours?" No wonder I needed a bathroom. "You couldn't have found somewhere more comfortable for me."

"As I said, I didn't expect you to be out for so long. I just kept thinking you would wake up soon and I had work, so I kind of forgot that you were even there and the time just flew by," he said, waving his hand around to emphasize his point.

"That makes me feel special." I grimaced, taking a sip of the water. It didn't taste like I was being poisoned.

"Why am I here?" I asked.

"Have a seat," the businessman went to his chair behind the desk and gestured to the one opposite.

I sat down carefully. "Are you going to kill me?" I asked.

He smiled. "You are very direct," he said. "I don't intend to kill you but as you are here, I do have some questions for you." It could just have been my sensitive state but I think I noticed a slight emphasis on the word 'intend'.

"Can I go home?" I asked.

"No, not yet, I think we need to get to know each other better before you go home. This situation could be misinterpreted."

"Really?" I asked, trying very hard not to let the sarcasm through too much. Obviously I failed because he looked at me reprovingly.

"Of course, how do you think I feel? Through no fault of my own I've ended up with you in a precarious state for most of my day. I had plans that didn't involve babysitting an unconscious woman."

"From the sounds of it, you didn't put a great deal of effort into seeing to my comfort," I said scathingly, and wanted to kick myself. Obviously whatever drugs had been injected into my system had completely shut down the self-preservation center of my brain.

"I need a bathroom," I said.

He looked at me with the expression of someone whose patience had reached the limit of normal humans but that I should be grateful that he had saint like levels available to him.

"Through here," he said tiredly, coming around the desk and helping me up. He seemed to have a bathroom attached to the office and gave me a small push through the door. I closed it behind me and heard him sigh through the door. Considering I was the one who had been drugged and kidnapped, he was definitely making a drama out of being the one who was the victim here. I looked around the bathroom for a window, or any other way of escape.

"There aren't any windows and no vents," the tired voice called through to me. "The only way out is through this door. Once we've had our little chat I'll take you back to your hotel myself."

I wondered if I could take him. I'm not particularly petite and thanks to an inability to diet for any length of time I had a bit of weight to me. Not much, but enough to ensure I never intend to wear a bikini. For several seconds I fantasized about taking him by surprise, but who was I kidding? At the moment, going to the bathroom seemed to be a huge task for me to accomplish. Taking on a man who didn't intend to kill me, but seemed like he could change his mind in a heartbeat, was completely out of the realms of possibility. After cleaning myself up in the bathroom, I opened the door to find him leaning against the door frame.

"Who are you?" I asked when I realized that I had no idea who this man was.

"You don't know?" he asked as he sat down behind his desk.

"I don't mean to offend you if I'm supposed to know you, but I honestly don't have a clue," I said.

"At least it makes us even," he said, "I have no idea who you are either. All I know is that my colleague saw you as a threat so decided to bring you here."

"Then why don't you ask him what was going through his head?" I said. "Because this whole thing is crazy. There is no reason for anyone to kidnap me."

"Really?" he said as he leaned forward on the desk and looked thoughtful. "You don't know the man who took you."

"No," I stuttered a bit and the man eyed me suspiciously.

"I saw him at a funeral that I went to yesterday. I'd never seen him before then and I have no idea why he would kidnap me."

"Maybe because you followed him to Vegas," the man ventured.

"I did not follow him. My friends decided to get married on impulse and I came with them. That is the only reason that I am in Las Vegas. I have no other reason to be here. I really have to say that I don't want to be here. I really just want to go home."

"How can I send you home?" he asked. "I have no idea who you are or where you live. You've been through a traumatic experience and are most likely still under the effects of some powerful drugs. It would be irresponsible of me to just let you out on the streets."

"You're telling me that you won't let me go because you are worried about me?" I was having trouble keeping the incredulity out of my voice.

"Of course," he said and I swear he looked as innocent as a newborn baby. "I have no other reason for keeping you here."

"Who are you?" I asked.

"You can call me Dominic, and you are?"

"Trudie," I said. If he wanted to keep to first names, so would I.

"Trudie," he said. "That's an unusual name."

I know Trudie is an unusual name. What is more unusual is it is short for Gertrude, just like my great grandmother. That is what happens when childbirth, drugs and emotional blackmail all come together in a perfectly played hand by my Grandma Rita. After what my mother refers to as 'the disaster', she refused to name my sister and brother until she had left hospital and had two weeks to think about it. Most importantly, my grandmother had been banned from making any suggestions.

"So, Trudie, how do you know Catarina Badal?" Dominic asked.

"I don't," I said. "I met her once the night she died and she didn't even speak to me. I was just attending her last show because a friend of mine was acting in it."

"So why were you at the funeral?" Dominic leaned back in his chair studying me intently.

"My friend wanted to go to the funeral and he wasn't in a good way so I went to support him, as a friend," I said.

"That is unfortunate," Dominic said. "My colleague thought you knew Catarina and that is why you were after him."

"He was wrong," I said. "I saw him at the funeral, I didn't even know he'd be in Las Vegas. Like I said, my friends decided to get married. They asked me to come to be the bridesmaid and best man. They got married but I hadn't slept the night before because I had been working, so I was really tired and I went back to my room. The next thing I know, I'm being grabbed by some scary looking guy and I wake up on your floor nine hours later if what you're telling me is true. My friends are going to be panicking by now. Why did he kidnap me?" I asked, curiosity getting the better of me.

"Unfortunately, my colleague is quite paranoid at

times," Dominic said. "Seeing you in Las Vegas so soon after seeing you at Catarina's funeral made him suspicious. He thought he should question you and made an impulse decision."

"He injected me with a drug to knock me out," I said slowly. "How could that be an impulse decision? No one would carry that kind of thing around with him."

Dominic inclined his head towards me. "As I said, he is quite paranoid and has some personality issues which are less than desirable in a civilized society. He carries tools of his trade wherever he goes, for those emergency situations, you understand."

All of a sudden I was grateful that I had ended up on Dominic's floor. I still didn't know what he had in store for me, but I was thinking that it had to be better than a man who went about his day carrying a syringe with a drug cocktail capable of rendering some random person unconscious within a few minutes.

"Why did he bring me to you?" I asked slowly, wondering if I really wanted to hear the answer.

"My colleague had attended the funeral on my behalf. Catarina and I had some unfinished business. Her unfortunate demise has caused me some issues. My colleague had offered to see if he could bring that business to a satisfactory conclusion."

"He wasn't able to, was he?" I said and once again I blamed the drugs when Dominic looked at me shrewdly.

"I have a feeling, Trudie, that you know more than you are telling me."

"I don't know anything," I said.

Dominic looked like he didn't believe me. All I could hear in my head was my Grandma Rita's voice telling me that it was sweet that I couldn't lie worth a damn, but one day that trait, that was so adorable when I was a kid, was going to get me in trouble. Looked like today was that day.

"I would suggest that it would be in your best interests if you were to tell me the truth. My colleague was not happy when I suggested to him that I be the one to speak to you. I believe he had his own questions for you, and as you've already surmised, he would be less likely to have my patience," Dominic said.

"I really don't know anything," I said. "I saw him at the funeral, and that was only because he kind of stood out. It was a really small funeral and he didn't quite look like he belonged. After the funeral I saw him talking to Catarina's assistant but I really did not know what was going on and I really didn't follow him here, I promise." Because promises always work with bloodthirsty gangsters. Dominic may have been trying to pass himself off as an ordinary businessman but the more time I spent in his company, the less safe I was feeling.

Dominic sighed, "Catarina and I were involved."

Of course they were, Catarina seemed to be involved with everybody, although I had to give her points for bravery. Just from the short amount of time I had spent with Dominic, even I could see that fooling around on him was its own special brand of stupid.

"I see you are aware of Catarina's reputation," Dominic smiled tightly.

I nodded, unwilling to open my mouth until I was sure the drugs were out of my system.

"We had been together for a few months and I was unaware of her true character. Until I found something that showed my trust in her had been misplaced," he said.

"You found the book," I said and clapped my hand over my mouth. I wasn't planning on removing it until these drugs were out of my system, because they were going to get me killed.

"What book?" asked Dominic curiously.

"Just a notebook that Catarina kept," I said, returning my hand to my mouth.

"Do you know what was in the notebook?" Dominic asked silkily.

I nodded.

"Care to tell me what was in this notebook." Dominic looked like his saint like patience had worn out.

I shook my head.

Dominic leaned over and pulled my hand from my mouth. "I think I'm going to have to insist," he said quietly, and the hand gripping my wrist let me know it was not a request.

"Catarina kept a book with a list of all her partners with ratings," I said hurriedly.

For the first time since I had met him I could see Dominic showing some emotion other than disinterested civility. Anger seemed to pulse from him and I started to be very afraid of the man in front of me. The grip on my wrist tightened and I tried to pull it away.

Dominic let go of my wrist and sat down. "My, I always knew Catarina liked life a bit wild. I just never realized how close to the edge she liked to play."

I rubbed my wrist. That red mark was going to bruise.

"Have you seen this book?" Dominic asked.

"No," I said. "As far as I know the police have it. I've just heard about it."

"You would think I'd learn my lesson not to trust a pretty face," said Dominic quietly. "Unfortunately there are some women who make fools of us all."

I sat there quietly. No way was I opening my mouth, because obviously I no longer had any control over what was coming out of it.

"You wouldn't play with a man like that, would you?" Dominic asked.

I shook my head.

"You wouldn't steal from him either, would you?"

I shook my head again.

"I wouldn't say I trusted her exactly, but I gave her more leeway than I would usually give my women. She was just intoxicating and she knew the exact way to get a man's attention. Do you know what that's like?"

I knew what it was like, in a theoretical kind of way.

Unfortunately I missed that feminine seductive gene and the way I got Griffin's attention had been more along the lines of an accidental elbow to the face. Worked for him which could be a cause for concern if I thought about it too much.

"She was losing quite badly in one of my casinos when I met her and she charmed me in a way I hadn't felt in a long time."

I really wanted Dominic to stop talking. The more he talked, the less likely it was that I was getting out of here alive.

"Can I go now?" I asked quietly. "I obviously don't know anything."

"Are you sure you don't want to know what she stole from me?" Dominic asked.

"I really don't," I said. "The less I know, the happier I am going to be."

"See, that is being smart," Dominic said. "Catarina wasn't that smart, she was greedy. She stole a family heirloom from me. A necklace that had belonged to my mother, and she thought she could get away with it."

"Why don't you just tell the police and they could get it back for you," I said desperately.

"Men in my line of business do not go to the police, we solve our own problems," Dominic said seriously.

I shivered when I remembered that Catarina had died from a knife stuck in her back.

Dominic saw me shiver and smiled humorlessly. "Regardless of what you think of me, Trudie, you can believe that I wouldn't have killed Catarina. At least not until after I got the necklace back."

"But you didn't go to get the necklace yourself," I murmured. "You sent your colleague, and you yourself told me that he has personality issues that are not desirable in civilized society. What's to say that he didn't act impulsively?"

Dominic smiled tightly. "My colleague can be

impulsive, however, he does have a healthy sense of self-preservation. It's the reason he's survived so long in a dangerous industry. He was very aware that his first priority was to get my money and the necklace back. Catarina and I would settle our differences between ourselves at a later date, after she had paid back everything she owed me. I am a businessman, first and foremost."

I was feeling less and less safe around this businessman. I heard some noise coming from outside the office and the door was opened suddenly. I was surprised when three men walked in, two in police uniform and one with a detective badge on his belt.

"Detective Bradford, to what do I owe the pleasure of your company?" said Dominic calmly.

Detective Bradford smiled. "Caldwell, now this is a surprise. I've been looking for Trudie Eyre who was kidnapped earlier today, and I find her sitting here, at your desk."

Dominic smiled. "Of course you do. Trudie has only been conscious a short amount of time. I was just about to call you and let you know I'd found a poor unfortunate girl, unconscious on my property. I've had a doctor examine her and she has been declared healthy. We were just trying to work out how she ended up here. It is interesting though that you are looking for her so quickly. Usually missing people need to actually be missing for forty-eight hours before the police get involved. What is it about this young lady which entitles her to special treatment?"

"Can I go now?" I asked the Detective. I didn't know what game that Dominic was playing but I really wanted no part of it.

"Did this man kidnap you?" asked Bradford.

"Well, no," I said. "Another man kidnapped me. He stuck a needle in me with some weird cocktail of drugs and I woke up here."

"See, Detective," Dominic said. "Even your victim

thinks I'm innocent."

"No," I said thoughtfully, "I really don't."

"More proof that you are a very intelligent woman," said Dominic quietly. "I'd love to continue our chat someday."

"Please get me out of here," I whispered to Bradford.

"Caldwell, I would suggest you not go anywhere. I think I'm going to have some more questions for you."

"Of course not, Detective. You know my door is always open to you," Dominic said, leaning back in his chair, looking for all the world like the businessman he tried to project. I now knew better. Whoever Dominic was, he was a dangerous man.

Chapter Seventeen

Bradford pushed me forward but just as we went through the door, I stopped as Dominic called out.

"I look forward to seeing you again, Trudie."

I stiffened and started walking again. As Bradford settled me into the car, I could feel the nausea in my stomach starting up again.

"Are you okay, Trudie? You don't look too good," Bradford said.

"I was injected with a syringe. I don't know what was in it. I really think I need to go to a hospital."

Bradford swore. "Hold on, I'll get you there," he said, and I had to concentrate very hard to control my nausea as we flew through the Las Vegas streets heading for a hospital.

I just tried desperately to hang on and not throw up in the nice policeman's car. At the hospital, I discovered that Detective Bradford had the superpower of being able to talk a nurse into anything. I was immediately pushed through emergency and more needles were stuck into me to find out what kind of a cocktail of drugs my kidnapper carried around in his pocket on a regular basis. Bradford stayed with me for most of the time, until a female doctor came in and tactfully told him to get the hell out so she could do some more examinations. Photos were taken of my wrist, which as expected, had bruised, and my neck with the puncture mark. After the medical and forensic staff were finished with me, I lay back on the hospital bed and closed my eyes. Everything had happened so fast that I hadn't had much of a chance to process the fact that I had been kidnapped. My eyes started burning and I heard Bradford murmuring outside. He poked his head in the door.

"You up for visitors?" he asked.

I nodded, not trusting my voice and sat up in the bed. Crystal barreled into the room and threw herself at me.

"Oh my God," she said tearfully as she squeezed me hard. "We've been so scared. Are you okay? Please tell me you're okay."

"I'm fine, Crystal. I wasn't hurt, I'm okay," I said, patting her on the back.

She nodded into my chest and squeezed a little harder.

Edwin came up behind her and stroked my head. "You've got to stop scaring us like this," he said quietly. "We can't lose you."

I swallowed against the lump in my throat.

"Not that I'm complaining at all, but how did you guys know I was gone so fast?" I asked. "I thought I wasn't going to be missed until tomorrow morning."

"Crystal wanted to check on you when we found you'd moved out of the suite," Edwin said knowingly.

"I wanted you guys to have a good wedding night and I thought you might feel a little inhibited if I was in the suite. I just wanted to give you some privacy," I said.

"We figured," said Edwin, "Crystal wanted to tell you that you were an idiot, so we went to your room and found the door open and you weren't there."

"We went to the cops and they told us we had to wait forty-eight hours," Edwin said.

Crystal lifted her head and I could see tears streaked down her face.

"I called Griffin," she said quietly.

"Griffin knows?" I asked.

"Damn right Griffin knows," growled a voice from the doorway and there he stood. His clothes were rumpled, he looked tired and stressed and to me he was the most wonderful sight I had ever seen.

He stood by the bed and grabbed my hand. "New rule, you are not allowed out of my sight ever again," he said gruffly and then sat on the side of the bed and gathered me in his arms. I finally felt safe so I promptly burst into tears. While I was sobbing on Griffin's chest, I felt Edwin and Crystal kiss me on the head and say they'd be back in the morning. After what seemed like hours I finally ran out of tears and just let Griffin's warmth melt the cold block of fear which had been in my stomach since I'd opened the door to my hotel room.

"Feeling a bit better?" Griffin said roughly.

"I am," I said. "I don't think your shirt is going to recover though."

He pulled back and cupped the side of my face. "You scare the hell out of me," he said quietly. "You know that, don't you?"

"I'm sorry," I said, feeling the tears coming back.

"Oh, honey, it's not your fault that the thought of losing you terrifies me more than anything else possibly could."

"Really?" I asked.

"Yes, really," he said. "Are you ready to tell Bradford what happened?"

I nodded. "Not really," I said.

Griffin chuckled and got off the bed.

"Where are you going?" I said, hating the fear that I could hear in my voice.

"I'll just get Bradford, he's waiting outside the door. Don't worry, I'm not going anywhere," he said reassuringly.

When Griffin came back with Detective Bradford following, I could see how exhausted both men looked. It was the middle of the night and both looked like they were running on empty. Griffin sat again on the bed and Bradford settled into a chair.

"So," said Bradford, "I need you to tell me what happened."

I tried to concentrate. Already the day seemed to be a blur.

"I was in my room, ready to go to bed. I hadn't slept

the night before because I had been working and then Crystal and Edwin wanted to fly here to get married. I was so tired and I opened the door without checking. The guy from Catarina's funeral, the one who was threatening Peter was there. He grabbed me and held me against him while he injected me in the neck. I tried to fight him but he was too strong and I just couldn't get away." I could feel Griffin's hand tightening against mine. I looked up and could see the anger on his face. "I don't remember anything after that until I woke up on Dominic's floor."

"You mean Dominic Caldwell," interrupted Bradford.

"He only gave me his first name. He told me I'd been out for nine hours and that I'd ended up there because a colleague of his had made an impulse decision."

"That's one way of spinning it," muttered Bradford.

"From what he said, it seems Catarina Badal had stolen some necklace which belonged to his mother from him. Seems he was one of the men she was dating. She also owed him money from gambling debts. The guy who kidnapped me had been sent to the funeral to get back what she owed Dominic. When he saw me at the funeral and then in Las Vegas only a day later, it seems he panicked. He thought that I was following him and decided to kidnap me."

"Did Caldwell hurt you?" asked Bradford.

I lifted up my arm and pointed to the wrist. "He grabbed my wrist when I didn't want to tell him about the notebook that Catarina had."

Bradford looked confused.

"Catarina Badal had a notebook that listed and rated all of her lovers," Griffin supplied.

Bradford chuckled. "Dominic Caldwell would not have liked that one little bit," he said.

"Who is he?" I asked, the frustration evident in my voice.

Bradford leaned back in the chair. "Dominic Caldwell is a very powerful man who does not believe that the law applies to him. Most of his businesses seem to be legitimate but there are some areas which various law enforcement agencies are convinced are not so legal. Caldwell is powerful enough not to be bothered by what we believe. It is probably the reason that he could be so mixed up in your kidnapping and still not have any concern at all. Unfortunately, that bruise on your wrist is not going to be nearly enough for a conviction. I don't think anyone is going to be willing to try to prosecute him. If we take him down, we want to take him down for something big."

"So, they get away with it," I said bitterly. "He wasn't going to let me go until I gave him answers. Doesn't that make him part of the kidnapping?"

"He's saying he was concerned for your wellbeing and was just ensuring that you were okay," Bradford said. "It's classic your word against his and he has deeper pockets and far better lawyers. However, we do have security footage of one Roger D'Angelo carrying you out of your hotel, which gives us a better chance against him. We're looking for him at the moment but he seems to have gone to ground."

I must have looked worried because Griffin squeezed my hand. "Don't worry, I won't let anything happen to you," he said.

"Speaking of which, Griffin, you want to pop out of the room for a bit," Bradford said casually.

Griffin's head snapped up.

"I need to speak to her without you hanging around," Bradford said gently. "You know I do, buddy. Why don't you go and grab something to eat. I won't leave her until you get back."

Reluctantly, Griffin stood up and kissed me on the head. "Don't upset her," he growled at Bradford and stalked out of the room.

Bradford watched him leave and then turned around and looked at me thoughtfully.

"What?" I asked.

"Just wondering what it is about you that has Griffin tied in knots. I know the man and until today I could have sworn that there was nothing on this Earth that could make him lose his cool. Then today I get him on the phone telling me that some woman has not been where she is supposed to be and he wants me to get my ass on the case straight away while he flies from LA. He almost lost it completely when we found that security footage of you being carried out by D'Angelo."

"How do you know Griffin?" I asked.

Bradford shrugged. "Met him a few years ago at one of those interagency conferences. Kept in touch since then, helped each other out when cases crossed over between Vegas and LA. Is there anything else Dominic Caldwell said to you that could help me build a case against him?"

I shook my head. "He didn't make any threats as such and he only really got angry when he found out about the book and that Catarina had been seeing other men."

Bradford grinned, "I can't see him taking that too well. He's not the kind of man that likes to lose to anyone."

"So how did you find me?" I asked.

Bradford shrugged. "Lucky break more than anything else. We managed to track D'Angelo to Caldwell's house using traffic cams but we lost him after that. I went to Caldwell to see if D'Angelo had been there. Wasn't really expecting to find you chatting with him."

Bradford stood up. "I'll send Griffin back in, I'm pretty sure he's right outside the door waiting for me to go."

"Thanks," I said. "And thank you for finding me."

Bradford was right and Griffin came back into the room still looking worried. When he sat down on the bed next to me, I raised a hand and pushed back the hair from his forehead.

"I'm okay," I said, hating the look in his eyes. "You should go and get some sleep. I'll be fine here. I'll see you in the morning."

"I'm not going anywhere," Griffin said as he settled in the chair beside the bed. "I'll stay right here. Not the first time I've sat in a hospital chair with you."

I shuffled over on the bed and patted the space beside me. "Lie down here, there's enough room for the two of us," I said.

He toed off his shoes and got on the bed, gathering me in his arms.

"This is nice," he said.

"Yes," I agreed.

As I drifted off to sleep, I felt safer than I ever had before.

Chapter Eighteen

Waking up the next morning, I panicked at first as I forgot where I was. Turning my head, I found Griffin watching me.

"You know you're beautiful," he said softly and I remembered why this man took up so much of my emotional energy.

At that moment a nurse bustled in.

"It's about time you two woke up. Doctor's going to be here in a second and this isn't a honeymoon suite. You're lucky I was on duty. Most of the other nurses would have kicked your behind out of that bed and out of this hospital.

"Yes, ma'am," said Griffin, stretching his long frame as he got up out of the bed.

"What is it about men that think they will get out of trouble if they just say, 'yes ma'am'," the nurse grumbled.

Griffin's cell phone rang and he indicated he'd be stepping out of the room. The nurse closed the door firmly after him.

"Now, young lady, if you want to get out of here I would suggest a quick shower and getting dressed. Nothing tells a doctor that you're good enough to get out of hospital if you look like you are more prepared to face the day than he is."

Wholeheartedly agreeing to the sentiment, I had a quick shower and threw on some clothes that Crystal had brought me the night before. Walking out of the bathroom, I found Griffin standing in the room, his smile approving as it looked me up and down, although it darkened at the bruising on my neck from the rough entry of the needle and the obvious bruising on my wrist.

"Bradford just called. They've managed to pick up

D'Angelo," he said.

"Great." I smiled.

"I'm just going to go change my clothes. I'll only be a half an hour and I'll be right back," he said.

I walked up to him and wound my arms around his waist and laid my head on his chest.

"I'm fine," I said. "Go do whatever it is that you need to do. The doctor will take a while to get here and then the paperwork to get me out will take a while. Go have a shower, get changed and I'll see you when you get back here and then we can go home to LA."

"Is that what you want to do?" asked Griffin.

"Like you would not believe," I said.

"I'll be right back," he said, kissing me on the forehead.

After the doctor had arrived and pronounced me fit to leave, I sat on the bed and waited for the discharge paperwork to be completed. Hearing a noise at the door, I looked up to see Dominic Caldwell in my doorway with a large bunch of flowers and that unnerving smile of his.

I scrambled off the bed and reached for the nurse's buzzer.

"Please don't, Trudie. I'm not here to hurt you," he said. "I just wanted to make sure you were recovering from yesterday's unpleasantness."

"Which part?" I asked. "The part where I was kidnapped, or when I spent nine hours on your floor and could have died. Or maybe the part where you wouldn't let me go when I woke up until you got the answers you wanted."

Dominic smiled. "I know that in the cold light of day you may be feeling some anger towards the situation, but I had hoped that some time and space would give you a bit of clarity."

"Your colleague is with the police," I said.

"Yes, it was suggested to him that his actions were a little badly thought out and that it would be in everyone's best interests that he take responsibility for them. A plea deal will be worked out and he will be punished according to the laws of the state," Dominic said.

As if he suddenly remembered, he put the flowers on the end of the bed, being careful not to approach me as if I was a highly strung thoroughbred who would bolt if he got too close.

"These are for you, I hope you like them."

I barely looked at them. Something was happening here and all I knew was I did not like it at all.

"All expenses you have incurred while in Las Vegas have been taken care of," he said, that smooth voice scraping over my already jangled nerves.

"Why?" I croaked, wanting to shrink back as he walked slowly towards me, but standing still and holding my ground.

Dominic reached forward and grabbed my hand gently, raising it and pulling back on the sleeve to show the mark that he had put on my wrist yesterday. His thumb gently stroked the bruise.

"I do not apologize often. In my world it is seen as a sign of weakness." He looked me in the eyes. "But for this, I am sorry. My pride was damaged and I allowed that to hurt you. For this and no other reason I am in your debt for the hurt I have caused you."

I pulled back my hand. I badly wanted to step back because he was way too close, but I didn't want to appear weak and afraid, even though I really was.

"I don't want you to be in my debt. I don't want you anywhere near me. I want to leave this city and never think about what happened here again."

"The thing is," Dominic continued as if I hadn't spoken, "you've piqued my interest. You're not like the women I usually meet."

Oh this was bad, very, very bad. I can honestly say that I did not want to pique this man's interest at all. I was getting to the point where I was going to say to hell with my pride and run out of the room when a voice came from the doorway.

"Would you like to explain what you are doing here, Mr Caldwell?"

Griffin was standing there and I almost sagged with relief. He had cleaned up and he filled the doorway with his size and cop demeanor. The frown on his face was directed solely at Dominic. Most people I knew, at least felt a little trepidation when having Griffin's cop face focused at them. Dominic just smiled.

"I was just making sure that Trudie was fully recovered after her traumatic day yesterday." He turned to me. "I look forward to the next time we meet," he said smoothly and walked out, not even skirting around Griffin.

Griffin's forehead furrowed. "What's going on here?" he barked at me.

"You're yelling at me," I said. "He came in here and freaked me out and you're yelling at me."

Griffin ran his hand over his face. "I'm sorry."

Look at me, getting apologies from two men in five minutes. There has got to be a prize for that.

"What did he want?" asked Griffin.

"He wanted to give me flowers, pay my bills and tell me I'd piqued his interest. All of which are guaranteed to freak me out, so can we go, before I have a complete meltdown and they decide to keep me here indefinitely," I said.

"Crystal and Edwin are waiting downstairs in the cab," Griffin said. "Bradford called, D'Angelo is taking a plea deal so you don't need to do anything. I think we should get out of here before anything else happens," he said, grabbing my bag.

Following Griffin out, I looked at the flowers which were still lying on the bed and shivered. Dominic had arranged everything, just as he said, and I had a very bad feeling that he wasn't finished with me yet.

Chapter Nineteen

Walking into my home, I wanted to drop to my knees and kiss the floor. After a flight that had Griffin, Crystal and Edwin watching over me as if I was going to fall apart on them, I was happy to be in my own space again.

"Where did you want your bag?" asked Griffin.

Of course I wasn't alone. Crystal and Edwin had managed to realize that I might need some alone time right about now. Griffin hadn't quite worked it out yet and with the way he dropped himself onto my couch, it looked like he was taking seriously his threat not to let me out of his sight.

"So," I said as I dropped on the couch opposite him. "Is there a plan from here or are we just winging it?"

"Oh, there's a plan," said Griffin and jumped up at a knock on the door.

I did not like the sound of that and I realized how much when Griffin came back into the living room, followed by his father who was carrying a small duffel bag.

"What are you doing here, Lee?" I asked with trepidation.

"I have to go to work," said Griffin. "So Dad is going to stay and keep an eye on you."

I looked at the two men, the expressions on their faces so similar. "Can I please speak with you a moment, in private," I said.

Griffin followed me to my bedroom and when I closed the door he looked around the room.

"Took you long enough to get me in here," he grinned.

"I am not having your dad babysitting me," I hissed.

"And of course it has to be an argument," Griffin sighed. "Yesterday you were kidnapped. Dominic

Caldwell, who despite appearances is not a very nice man, has taken a frightening interest in you. I need to go to work today because I have a feeling once I can solve the Catarina Badal case, you may be taken out of the firing line. And believe me, sweetheart, at the moment that is the thing I want more than anything in the world. I can't do my job if I am worrying the entire day about you. If I bring anything but my A game to work, Ramos is going to have my hide. I am asking you, for my peace of mind, let my dad keep you company today."

I hated when people argued logically. It totally took the wind out of my sails.

"I don't like feeling like I'm not in control of my life, Griffin. I really don't react well when I feel someone is taking that away from me."

Griffin took me in his arms "I know, and that independent streak in you makes me hot."

"I thought it annoyed you," I said, looking up at him and smiling.

"Oh it does that too," said Griffin with an answering smile.

He dipped his head and slanted his lips over mine. I didn't even bother fighting the feeling that ran all the way down to my toes. In no time the kissing had turned passionate and I could feel him moving me over to the bed as he started kissing me across my jaw and down my neck. Sanity prevailed and I pulled away.

"Your dad is right outside this door," I gasped.

Griffin groaned. "I really want to pick this up soon," he said.

"We will," I said, "but you have to go to work."

Griffin gave me another quick and hard kiss on the mouth. "I'll see you tonight," he said. "We'll have dinner together, just the two of us with no interruptions, and then we're taking off right about here," he said, holding onto my hips and curling them into his body.

"Just the two of us," I repeated, feeling a little

lightheaded.

"You might want to do those buttons up," he said, glancing at my chest as he tucked in his shirt. Seems we'd both got a little busy during the interlude.

Griffin left, leaving me facing his father who looked at me with a bemused smile.

"So," I said, "how are you doing, Lee?"

"Fine, heard you went and got yourself kidnapped," he growled.

"I did not get myself kidnapped. I was kidnapped," I said patiently.

"So, we'll be putting it in the, 'it could only happen to you', pile," said Lee.

"Oh this is going to be fun today," I said. "Do you want a coffee?"

"That would be lovely," said Lee.

Busying myself with the coffee machine, Lee sat himself down at my table and studied me intently.

I put his coffee in front of him. "What?" I said tiredly.

"Just looks like you two are moving along with your relationship," he said as he kept his eyes firmly fixed on the coffee cup.

Lee Griffin was an ex-cop. I had met him before and at first had decided that he hardly spoke at all. There seemed to be one topic where this did not hold true. Lee had an inordinate amount of interest in Griffin's and my relationship. I had told him before to butt out but he seemed to be unable to help himself. I knew there was no way that he would ask his son these questions, but he seemed to have no problem with dragging me across the coals every time I met him.

"We're sorting things out," I conceded.

"You taking off the way you did was not good for his temper. The boy was like a bear with a sore head. He doesn't have the nicest of dispositions to begin with. When he saw that photo of you with the little pop star, I thought he was going to throw a coronary," Lee said conversationally.

"You're aware that the photo was just a media beat up," I said dryly, settling in with my own coffee. I figured if I was going to get grilled by my new boyfriend's father, I was going to need the strong stuff.

"Knew that from the second I saw it. Jake did too. Just didn't make him happy, seeing as how you'd walked away from him and you seemed to be enjoying the high life."

I snorted. "I was dragging a bratty, spoiled teenager out of a strip club. Trust me, I wasn't living the high life," I said.

"Do you like your job?" Lee asked curiously.

I thought back to the night with Blythe Stanton and to some of the people I had met while working for Monique.

"It does have its moments," I said, smiling. "No job is perfect and there are some days when it drives me crazy, but I would definitely say it has been worth it. Besides, I met Griffin through my job. If I'd had an office job somewhere, we may never have met."

Lee snorted. "The way you attract trouble, sweetheart, it was just a matter of time before you crossed Jake's path."

I wanted to argue, but really, there are some truths which you can't argue against.

Finishing off his coffee, Lee announced, "I've got errands to run and you're coming with me."

"What if I've got stuff to do?" I asked.

"Then we do that first," said Lee, very calmly and I was reminded of the way Griffin was, calm and competent. Well that's how he was when he wasn't dealing with me.

I shrugged, knowing when I'd been beaten. "Where do you need to go?" I asked.

"Drugstore," Lee muttered. "It's lousy getting old, spend half your life in the drugstore."

Wandering through the drugstore waiting for Lee to do his shopping, I ended up in an aisle of condoms. All of a sudden I started thinking. Griffin had given a strong indication that he wanted to have sex and considering the way I melted every time he touched me, I was obviously on board with the idea. It had been a long time since I'd had sex. I started panicking. As far as I knew, we were going to be at my house. What if he didn't have condoms? Maybe I should have some on hand. I started looking at the different brands and sizes. I grabbed a box and looked at it, then saw another one and pulled that down from the shelf as well. Just to be on the safe side I should get some, I decided. Now the question was, which ones? All of the boxes seemed to promise some out of this world experience. I had no idea of sizes or which brand was best. What would Griffin prefer? Maybe I should just close my eyes and pick one.

"I'm ready," said Lee as he walked up to me. "Do you need to get anything?"

You would think that the most embarrassing experience would be the moment you are looking at condoms, and the father of the man you are planning on using those condoms with stands next to you and asks you what you are doing. It isn't. The truly mortifying moment is three seconds later when he realizes what you're looking at and why, clears his throat, mutters that he'll wait for you outside and bolts for the closest exit. I was not going to be able to look Lee in the eyes for the rest of the day, maybe never. I grabbed the nearest box and took it to the counter. Paying for it, I didn't notice a gentleman in a suit standing by a side exit watching me intently until I nearly ran into him.

"Sorry," I muttered as I tried to step around him, still caught up in my humiliation.

The man in the suit put a hand on my elbow and, before I could wrench it away, he said, "Miss Eyre, Mr Caldwell would like to speak to you," in a low voice.

No way was that going to happen. I'd already spent far more time with Mr Caldwell than I ever wanted to. I must have telegraphed my intentions because my captor's grip tightened on my arm.

"Miss Eyre, you will be coming with me. It is your choice how it happens but I really don't think you want a repeat of yesterday do you?"

I looked into his eyes. He was serious. This man was going to take me to Dominic Caldwell, no matter what. I really didn't want that meeting to begin with me being unconscious again. I looked around but he had grabbed me in a part of the store which couldn't be seen from the front. Nobody was in this part of the store and I had been pulled in close as my captor tucked me into his side. We looked for all the world like a couple, except for the fact I could feel a gun in a shoulder holster against me. I went with him out the side door, hoping that Dominic Caldwell still did not intend to kill me.

Chapter Twenty

Parked outside in a laneway was a limousine. My kidnapper opened the door and pushed me in, none too gently. I dropped my bag as I fell into the seat and the box of condoms rolled out. Dominic Caldwell leaned over and picked up the box and held them out for me.

"For you and the good detective, I presume," he said, a smile crossing his face.

I snatched the box out of his hand and stuffed it in my handbag.

"None of your business," I snapped as I felt the blush work its way up my neck and across my face.

Dominic laughed as I settled into my seat, trying desperately to portray a casual, sophisticated demeanor. There's a reason that look never works for me.

"It's good to see a woman who blushes for a change," he said. "The women I usually spend my time with are too worldly to ever blush."

"Lucky you," I said through gritted teeth as my face felt warmer.

He traced a finger down my cheek. "I may be missing out," he said quietly.

I froze. Of all the things I was expecting, I had to admit this was not one of them.

"What do you want from me?" I croaked. You would think after being kidnapped for the second time in twenty-four hours I could at least be a bit calmer about it.

"We never got to finish our chat," said Dominic. "Unfortunately we kept getting interrupted."

"So you decided to kidnap me," I said.

"I am not kidnapping you," Dominic sighed as if repeatedly having to explain things to a small child.

"Actually," I said, "today really counts as a kidnapping.

Thug with a gun and threats definitely equals kidnapping."

"I told Robert that I needed to speak to you. He may have got a little enthusiastic with the execution of that order."

I really wish Dominic hadn't used the term execution.

"I was with my boyfriend's father in that drugstore," I warned. "The second he can't find me, you're going to have the LAPD combing the streets looking for me."

"You do seem to excite extreme loyalty in people," Dominic said, just as calmly. "It doesn't matter, as soon as we've finished our discussion I will take you wherever you want to go. I wouldn't dream of hurting you in any way."

"I don't know why you want to talk to me," I said, letting the frustration show. "I didn't know Catarina at all."

"But you know about her," prompted Dominic. "And I've been looking into your past, Trudie. You seem to make a habit of gaining information about people."

"I've heard things," I admitted, "but I don't know how much of it is true."

"Tell me everything you know, or have heard," Dominic commanded.

"Okay," I said, deciding that being agreeable may actually get me home in time to use those condoms.

"From what I've heard, Catarina Badal used people. I spoke to someone from her high school and they said everything she did in life she got from cheating or conning someone, if not outright stealing. In college she seduced a professor and tricked him into marrying her by faking a pregnancy."

"She's married?" Dominic asked.

"Yes, she refused to divorce the guy because that would mean losing part of her money under California law. That and I've been told she got some sort of perverse pleasure out of preventing her husband from getting on with his life. I've been told that there are doubts that the films she won awards for were actually her work. According to the person I spoke to, she didn't have an original thought in her head. My understanding is she was beautiful and full of personality. She made the most of those two attributes. Oh, and the only thing she seemed to actually care about was her cat," I said, without taking a breath.

Even though I had only known Dominic for a very short period of time, I knew he was a man who prided himself on his control. In this moment I saw him look angry and I was really afraid, because I knew I was seeing the very bad and very dangerous man that Griffin had warned me about. I dropped my eyes to my hands, clasped in my lap. I didn't think he would be very impressed at me witnessing this loss of control. I tried picturing the funeral and anyone else that I had spoken to about Catarina and her death.

"Wait a second." A vague memory teased itself through my mind. "Do you have a picture of the necklace?"

Dominic pulled a photo of the necklace from his jacket pocket and passed it over to me. Looking at it, I got a picture in my head of the day of the funeral. All of a sudden, the memory that had been twisting just out of sight, hit me.

"Oh no," I said and Dominic straightened.

"You know where the necklace is, don't you? You've remembered seeing it."

I gulped, wishing desperately that I wasn't the one telling him this.

"Well, where is it?"

I dropped my head. "She turned it into a cat collar."

"What?" The deadly tone in Dominic's voice made me wish very much that I didn't have to be the one to tell him this.

"This emerald and the two rubies on this necklace, they look exactly like the stones on the collar that Catarina's cat had around her neck at the funeral. I thought they were rhinestones. I've never seen stones that big that were real. I figured it was one of those ostentatious cat collars people get that are more costume jewelry."

"Are you telling me that my mother's priceless emerald and ruby necklace, which has been in our family for generations, has been pulled apart and turned into a cat collar?" Dominic's voice seemed to increase in volume the further along in that sentence that he went.

I nodded.

"Are you sure?"

"I guess it could be a copy," I said hopefully.

"But you don't think so, do you?" said Dominic.

I shook my head. I really wish that I could say that it was something else and there was a part of me that rebelled at the thought. What kind of person would steal a priceless necklace and turn it into a cat collar? I could see that it was lucky that Catarina was dead already because if the look on Dominic's face was anything to go by, she wouldn't have been long for this world anyway.

"So, can you drop me off now?" I ventured.

"Afraid not," Dominic smiled. "So far, you have been invaluable to me. I might just keep you for a little bit longer if you don't mind."

"You really need to learn to understand the word, no," I said seriously.

"Maybe you're right." He shrugged. "I just don't often hear it."

"This is kidnapping," I said.

"Were you dragged in here? Is there any evidence that you are here against your will?" he questioned.

"The fact that I'm with you is evidence that I am here against my will, because there is no other reason for me to be breathing the same air that you are. I was dragged by your thug in here and he threatened to do what the guy yesterday did to me."

Dominic shrugged. "He may have been a little overenthusiastic in his interpretation of my request."

"Considering how often your people misinterpret your requests, I would really suggest that you take a course in communication, because there may be people out there who are not as forgiving as I am." I went through my purse and grabbed my cell.

"What are you doing?" Dominic said silkily.

"I'm calling Detective Griffin and letting him know where I am. If you don't want this to be classified as a kidnapping I would suggest you just sit there and let me do what I want. If you don't, the second this door opens, I will kick and scream at the top of my lungs, so the situation will satisfy even your narrow interpretation of the word."

Dominic grimaced as I punched in Griffin's number.

"Where the hell are you?" So much for niceties, looked like Griffin really didn't handle stress well. Everybody kept telling me about him having this ice cold, calm personality. Frankly I didn't see it, or maybe more to the point, I didn't inspire it.

"Dominic Caldwell felt that we needed to finish the chat we were having when you interrupted us at the hospital."

"You're with Dominic Caldwell?" Strangely, Griffin sounded like he couldn't quite believe what he was hearing.

"Looks like it."

Dominic was smiling as he sat across from me.

"Are you there willingly?" asked Griffin slowly as if trying to assimilate my change in circumstances.

"We were just discussing that," I said. "We seem to have differing interpretations on what constitutes willing."

"Where are you?" Griffin was starting to get that tone in his voice that I knew was a prelude to a blow up. "I'm coming to get you now."

"Could be a little bit of a problem, it seems my expertise is being requested." I couldn't help but feel a little bit smug.

"Your expertise in what?" Griffin sounded doubtful. I chose not to be insulted.

"I have no idea. Seems there is a missing necklace that

Catarina stole from Dominic Caldwell and I may have an idea where it is. From my understanding of the situation I would say that we're going looking for a cat."

I could almost hear Griffin grinding his teeth. "Just so we're clear, you are currently in the company of a man who is, as we speak, on the radar of several law enforcement agencies, and the two of you are searching for a cat."

That pretty much summed up my day. Hearing him say it so calmly, I could see why he was having a bit of trouble getting his head around it.

"I just wanted you to know that I'm safe and not to worry," I said.

"Don't worry," Griffin echoed. "Are you out of your mind? I want you to tell me where you are right now so I can get you."

I looked out the window of the car. "At the moment I'm in a limo heading down the freeway. I'm not entirely sure where we are headed." I looked at Dominic expectantly and he just shrugged. "Looks like it is a mystery trip but Dominic assures me that as soon as we find the cat he will deliver me home." Dominic shrugged again and I gave him a dirty look.

"If I'm not home or don't call you in an hour, come looking for me," I muttered and turned the phone off.

"So," I said as I settled back in my seat. "We're looking for a cat."

Dominic sighed in disgust as if suddenly realizing what a ridiculous situation he was in. "To be perfectly honest, we're heading for the reading of Catarina's will."

"Why?" I asked, a little confused.

"Ostensibly it is because, thanks to her gambling debts, I am considered a creditor to Catarina's estate. I normally wouldn't attend these things."

"Let me guess, you have colleagues who take care of them."

Dominic smiled faintly. "Yes, I do. However, this

situation is different in that I was hoping to get a chance to find the necklace, so I planned to attend today's reading myself. Of course, after the debacle that occurred because I sent D'Angelo to find the necklace, I am beginning to realize that I may be delegating too much to people who aren't able to handle the responsibility."

I couldn't help but agree with him.

Chapter Twenty-One

The lawyer's offices were spacious with more than enough room to handle a reading. It looked empty though with only Catarina's assistant and husband in attendance. Peter started with surprise when he saw Dominic walk into the room and his brow furrowed with confusion at the sight of me coming in with him. I was right there with him. How I ended up in this drama was going to require a flow chart and a white board when Griffin demanded an explanation, which I knew he was going to do.

Sitting down next to Dominic, I could hear the low volume yowling. Looking around, I saw the cat carrier sitting on the ground next to Peter's chair. I should have realized that Peter had it because his skin had once again taken on that blotchy look it seemed to permanently have around Cleopatra. He was also sniffing and his eyes were watering horribly. I elbowed Dominic and, using my head, indicated in the direction of the cat carrier. The lawyer entered the room and sat down at his desk. Clearing his throat, he started talking.

"As you are aware we are here today to discuss the final disposal of the estate of Catarina Badal. As executor of the will I have been tasked to finalize these matters. I won't read the will, copies will be made available to you. Firstly, I needed to address the matter of the creditors. Mr Caldwell has a sizable interest due to debts incurred by Miss Badal."

The lawyer shuffled some papers and his assistant passed them to Dominic. "As you can see, all debts are covered."

Dominic barely glanced at the papers. "This doesn't address the necklace that was wrongly appropriated by Catarina," he said mildly.

The lawyer cleared his throat, his nervousness apparent.

"A thorough inventory has been made of Miss Badal's holdings. The necklace you are speaking of has not been found anywhere."

Dominic was silent for a moment and I could see that everyone was becoming uncomfortable. "I have reason to believe that Catarina pulled the necklace apart and repurposed it."

The lawyer looked perplexed. "We found nothing in her jewelry that even looked similar," he said.

Dominic sighed. "Did anyone bother to look at the cat collar?"

The assistant looked horrified. See, I wasn't the only one. I know I can be accused of not being a cat lover but the thought of a precious necklace stolen and turned into a cat collar was ridiculous. I mean, who did that? Everyone looked at the cat cage and, as if she realized she had become the center of attention, the cat kicked up the volume.

Peter looked at the cage in distaste.

"I'm going to need help to remove the collar," he said. "I can hold the cat but someone else will need to take it off."

I looked at Dominic in his very expensive suit. He shrugged at me. I didn't see him volunteering in a hurry. I walked over to Peter.

"Let's get this over and done with," I muttered.

With practiced movements, Peter undid the cage door, grabbed both front paws in one hand and the scruff of the cat in the other. Pulling her out, he clamped her body under his arm, all while sneezing helplessly with tears streaming from his eyes.

"Get it now," he wheezed.

Working quickly, I reached up and undid the cat collar. Whipping it off, I shouted, "done," triumphantly and Peter shoved the cat back in the cage and closed the door. He then sat down heavily in his chair and pulled out a box of tissues. He started mopping up his eyes and nose, while his face started swelling to an alarming degree. I handed the collar over to Dominic who, despite the fact he had got the gems from the necklace back, looked like he badly wanted to kill somebody. I didn't blame him really. From the look of it, Catarina had pried the gems from their setting and glued them haphazardly on a relatively thick leather collar in a demented crafting exercise.

"Do we know where the setting is?" Dominic's voice was pitched low and the threatening tone made me take an involuntary step back.

I was obviously not the only one who felt the threat because the lawyer, who was already nervous, was sending off panic vibes that could be felt through the room.

"Now that we know the necklace is no longer whole, we will go through all her belongings and see if we can find the setting."

Dominic pinned him with a look that emphasized the point that he better not fail.

The lawyer cleared his throat nervously. "Can we continue?"

Dominic nodded and sat down again. I dropped down in the seat next to Peter, still a bit concerned that his wheezing had not stopped.

"Do you have something to help?" I whispered.

Peter sneezed. "No, I'm getting anti-allergy shots but they don't seem to be working yet."

"If you're finished," the lawyer pinned both of us with a look. I felt like a kid in school being reprimanded by the teacher.

"Sorry," I said weakly. Peter just sneezed again.

"As to the rest of the estate, my instructions are that it is to be liquidated and put into a trust. This trust is to be administered solely for the maintenance of Catarina's cat, Cleopatra. Cleopatra is to remain in the care of Peter Nolan and he will be paid a stipend of five thousand dollars a year out of the trust to care for the cat. Other than that, the trust will only allow money for certain expenses. Upon the death of Cleopatra, she is to be interred with Catarina's body and the trust will be dissolved and donated to a variety of animal shelters.

I looked around. Evan didn't look like he cared at all that he had been left out of the will, but then for him the main benefit was that he no longer had Catarina in his life. Dominic had a bored expression on his face that morphed into anger every time he saw that stupid cat collar. Peter looked like he was in massive amounts of pain but there was a disbelief to his features as he shakily stood up.

"What about the royalties for the movies?" he asked.

"They are part of the estate so they go into the trust." The lawyer barely looked up at Peter.

"But I wrote them. She promised that I would get the royalties and credit if she died."

Everyone looked at him, surprised.

"What do you mean, Peter?" I asked, gently trying to calm him down.

"I wrote the screenplays, but nobody was going to give me the time of day. Catarina had the contacts, she had the look, so we agreed that she would present them as hers but once they were made she would help me get ahead, so I could make my own movies."

"She never did that, did she?" I'd learned enough about Catarina Badal that I knew she never did anything for anyone except for that cat of hers.

"I wrote two movies for her and they got all those awards, and all that money and I never saw any of it."

"Why did you stay with her?" I put my hand on his shoulder.

"She said she loved me. She said she used all the other men in her life, that I was the only one for her, that we were perfect for each other. She said if I was her assistant, no one would ask questions and I could be with her always."

135

Peter looked completely lost. Evan was watching the situation with a complete lack of concern. In that moment I knew that he couldn't have killed Catarina. She meant nothing to him. From the look of it, the murder had seemed a crime of passion, and there was no passion there whatsoever. Dominic was angry but his problem was more pride than anything else. It started to dawn on me that the one person who had the most passion when it came to Catarina was the one I was standing a little too close to. I took a small step backwards and, from the look in Peter's eyes, I could tell that he knew what I had just worked out.

"I'm so sorry," I said, just as the doors sprung open and Griffin strode into the room with Ramos right behind him. Griffin stopped and his jaw dropped at seeing me there.

Ramos was not quite so stunned.

"I don't believe it," she exclaimed when her eyes landed on me.

Griffin recovered quickly. "Peter Nolan, we would like to speak to you regarding the murder of Catarina Badal."

Peter froze momentarily and then he snapped into action. He grabbed me around the waist and hauled me towards him. Griffin stepped forward as Ramos pulled her gun.

"Step back," Peter said and I felt something sharp pressed against my throat.

Griffin froze. "This is a really bad idea," he growled but stepped back anyway.

"What are you doing, Peter?" I could feel a small trickle of blood going down my throat.

"It isn't fair," he said. "She was supposed to give me the money, she was supposed to tell everyone that I was the one who wrote those screenplays. Instead I get the cat that makes me sick all the time. Why would she do that to me? I was the one she loved."

"She didn't love anyone except herself," Dominic sounded like he was bored with the entire situation. "If you believed she loved you, you're a bigger idiot than the rest of us."

I glared at Dominic, I should have known that sooner or later he was going to get me killed.

"Peter, if you don't let me go, you are going to get hurt."

"You're going out with the cop. Tomas told me at the funeral. He won't do anything that will risk you getting killed."

I conceded on that point. Unfortunately Griffin wasn't the only one in the room with a gun. "See his partner, she doesn't like me very much right now. Griffin might hold off but she is likely to shoot me in the leg just to see me suffer."

I wish I had been lying but I could see the look in Ramos's eyes, and frankly, I could tell that my being here was just another in the long list of grievances she held against me.

"I loved her," he whispered, "and I hated her. She laughed at me, I wanted to stop her laughing at me."

"Did you kill her?" I kept my eyes on Griffin because it was the only thing keeping me going at the moment.

"Yes," whispered Peter.

"Are you going to kill me?" I said, my voice seizing up with fear.

"No," said Peter.

"Then please let me go. If you don't, things are going to get worse than they are already."

I felt the knife drop away from my throat and Peter stepped back. Griffin and Ramos raced forward and Peter was thrown to the ground and handcuffed. Ramos still had her knee in Peter's back when Griffin grabbed hold of my arms.

"Are you okay? How deep is the cut?"

"Barely a scratch," I said quietly, my mind still trying to process what had happened.

He pulled me close and I wrapped my arms around his

waist.

"You can't keep doing this to me," he said.

"Not like I mean to," I mumbled into his chest.

"If you've finished babying her, we need to take this one down town," Ramos broke through the moment.

"Can you get home?" Griffin asked.

"Not a problem." I smiled at him, hoping it filled him with more confidence than it did me, especially as I didn't think he realized that ride was probably going to be with Dominic Caldwell.

"I'll meet you at your place when I've finished up," he whispered and gave me a brief kiss on the cheek.

Ramos puffed out her breath in disgust and dragged Peter towards the doorway. Griffin followed her.

"You do bring the excitement, don't you?" said Dominic, coming up behind me holding out a tissue.

"Maybe you should stop kidnapping me then," I said as I mopped at the small cut on my neck. "I need a ride home, and seeing as how I wouldn't be in this mess if it hadn't been for you, I think you owe me."

"Believe me," said Dominic, "from what I've learned about you in the last couple of days, sooner or later you would have been in the middle of this anyway."

Chapter Twenty-Two

Sitting in the limo, Dominic grimaced as he looked at the cat collar.

"I can't believe she did this. Do you have any idea what this necklace was worth?"

"To you maybe, Catarina obviously had a whole different set of priorities."

"You're judging me for being with her aren't you?" Dominic put the cat collar in his pocket.

"Like you would not believe," I said. "Don't get me wrong, I understand why Catarina was popular with men, she was gorgeous and vivacious. I met her, I know that every eye in the room went to her. What I don't understand is, you men were with her for far longer than a moment. Didn't you even bother to look at what was below the surface? I mean seriously, everything about this woman, except for the way she treated her cat, was selfish and narcissistic."

"I wasn't looking for anything deeper." Dominic defended himself. "Frankly, I didn't spend much time talking to her."

"Then you got out of the situation what you put in. You should be just as mad at yourself that she stole the necklace, because you let it happen."

Dominic nodded. I didn't think what I said made any difference so I just shrugged. Once we got to my apartment block, I got out of the car.

"I would say it was nice meeting you, but it really wasn't. The best I can do is hope that I never see you again," I said as I slammed the door.

I heard him laugh but by that point I was so annoyed I just headed up the stairs. Crystal and Edwin were outside the door of Crystal's apartment and they looked at me and took in the scratch on my neck and the blood that had dripped down onto my shirt.

I put my hand up. "Not a word, Peter is being charged with Catarina's murder. I'm okay and I just want to be left alone for twenty-four hours. No more emergency entries using my keys."

The two of them nodded, looking a little stunned, and I went into my apartment. Standing under a hot shower, I felt all the worries and fear washing away from me.

When Griffin knocked, I had finally calmed down. Opening the door I felt a little hesitant and hugged my arms around myself. Griffin looked concerned as he went past me into the living room and sat down on the couch.

"Do you want a drink or something?" I asked.

He shook his head and held a hand out to me. "Just let me hold you for a minute," he said, "I just need to know you're safe."

I felt tears in my eyes as I sat next to him and let him pull me into his arms.

"Gotta say, sweetheart, seeing you with a knife against your throat does not count as one of my better days," he muttered.

"Not one of mine either," I agreed. "So what happened with Peter?"

"Despite the fact I felt the need to toss him out of a moving car, he's been booked on Catarina's murder."

"How did you know?" I asked.

"We had a fingerprint off the knife he killed her with. Nothing special, just that and a healthy lot of suspicion. It wasn't until he grabbed you that we knew for sure that he had done it. Speaking of which, why were you at the will reading?"

I grimaced. "Would you believe that the reason Dominic Caldwell was after Catarina was because she stole a necklace from him while they were sleeping together? It belonged to his mother so he was not going to let it go. Unfortunately, when we were talking today, I remembered seeing the necklace, or what was left of it. Catarina pulled it apart and used the gems on a cat collar."

"You are kidding me, aren't you?" said Griffin.

"I wish I was."

"Caldwell got the necklace back?"

"Parts of it, hopefully the lawyer can find the rest."

Griffin grunted as he stroked his fingers down my arm. We sat there quietly for a few minutes.

"So my dad said you were looking at condoms." I could tell he was smiling.

"There's a sentence I never wanted to hear." I could feel myself blushing again.

"Did you buy some?"

I nodded.

"I need you to say it, sweetheart" he said gently, before he lowered his lips to mine. I reveled in the feeling

He raised his head. I looked into his eyes and I found some courage.

"Yes," I whispered.

About The Author

Leonie Gant started her writing career at the age of ten when she stuffed notes in her pencil case full of ideas for mysteries that Nancy Drew and the Hardy Boys should really have been solving. After years of watching mysteries play out in her head, she decided that writing them down was the best way to deal with them.

In her life away from writing, she is a voracious reader with not nearly enough time to make her way through all the books that she wants to read. She enjoys bushwalking, sewing and chocolate, possibly not in that order. She also believes in the value of trying new things, walking in the rain and enjoying every moment.

To find out more about Leonie Gant and her books
www.leoniegant.com

Discover other titles by Leonie Gant
Not Famous in Hollywood
Not Happily Married in Hollywood
Not Wanted in Hollywood
Not Suspicious in Hollywood
Not Forgotten in Hollywood